Home is the ultimate shelter.

To Luke & Naneice,

I hope you enjoy the book. Luke

I hope you enjoy the Book Naneice.

You both mean so much to me.

I appreciate your support.

Have a great glass of Pino when reading this.

JgM

LIVING IN LIMBO

Thomas Paul

A Lucky Bat Book

LIVING IN LIMBO

Copyright © 2013 by Gregory Benford

Cover Design: Shelly Fallon

ISBN 978-1-939051-44-8

LuckyBatBooks.com
10 9 8 7 6 5 4 3 2 1

ACKNOWLEDGMENTS

This was a very controversial book to write. While the story is fiction, I know many struggling homeowners (who prefer to remain anonymous) who have faced the situations featured in this book. I want to thank each and every one of them for their contributions. I feel your frustration and wish your experience had been different.

To my wife and literary agent, Bobbi, thank you for your knowledge and inspiration. We had numerous discussions planning, strategizing, and even disagreeing on how to proceed in writing this book. Overall, we make a great team and for that I am grateful!

I would like to thank Judy Wilson for her expert thoughts and advice. After you read my first draft and shared your thoughts, I got excited about the possibilities. And a special thank you to Laura Newman for sharing her writing experience and encouragement. I appreciate you introducing me to my publishing company, Lucky Bat Books.

I also will be forever grateful to Louisa Swann, my editor, who helped make this an interesting and exciting read. Additionally, a special thanks goes out to designer, Shelly Fallon, who did a tremendous job on the cover design and to my dear friend, Ed Jaster, who created concepts for the cover.

Lastly, I want to thank all my family and friends who have listened to me over the past year when I have been both frustrated and excited about the writing experience. I appreciate all of you being there for me throughout the years.

To the Reader:

There are real problems going on in this country, problems that no one seems to be addressing. This story springs from some of the injustice you hear about every day. The things I hear tear at my heart and so I did what every author does—I wrote about it. Though inspired by real life events, this story is a work of fiction, a cautionary tale in a world gone mad. The names, characters, businesses, places, events, and incidents are either the products of my imagination or used in a fictitious manner. Any resemblance to actual persons, living or dead, or actual events is purely coincidental.

Any legal references in this book are also used in a fictitious manner and should not be interpreted as federal- or state-mandated law or actual procedure.

PROLOGUE

I T WAS THREE O'CLOCK in the morning and rain pounded against the bedroom glass. The sound of nature letting loose with all its fury was deafening, but the storm wasn't what was keeping Barry Joseph awake. His mind raced in different directions. He needed to take action, but was unsure of what his next step should be. He looked over at his sleeping wife. How she could sleep with all that had been happening to them was something he couldn't understand. Maybe the stress was her sleeping pill; he knew how stress could drain a person's energy.

Barry couldn't stop thinking about the past. Memories swirled round and round through his mind. He clearly remembered how he'd handled Jay Lucas, the school bully, when he was a child. Once again, Barry was facing a bully, but he wasn't dealing with Jay Lucas now. This was not going to be a simple schoolyard fight. Today he was dealing with a much bigger force. Even though he was no longer a kid, the principle was the same. His father's advice from years ago still rang in his ears: "You're in a tough situation, but you can't let a bully get the best of you. You have to fight like a man. You may lose, but you have to give it your all. There is no other option."

Today's situation was not just about Barry's family, but his entire community. Yes, he would be putting everything he had at risk—his family, his business, and his reputation. But the slight chance he had of winning the battle and changing his situation would affect others as well. That made the battle worthwhile. Didn't it?

Barry's stomach rolled until he thought he would be sick. He was about to face a giant financial institution that held a massive amount of power over millions of Americans, an institution that provided more abuse than help. Someone had to do something instead of just sitting back and taking the abuse. What was going on was not right. The bank wasn't playing fair. They didn't really care about their customers, even though their advertising claimed they did. The customer service representatives wouldn't listen. Hell, most of them couldn't even communicate in English! How could he hope to get their attention? How do you communicate with someone who not only couldn't, but wouldn't listen to reason?

Barry staggered into the bathroom. Tears streamed down his face. He looked into the mirror and stared at the reflection of a broken man, a shell of the man he used to be only a few years ago. The stress had been too much. The pressure had mounted to the boiling point. He had to do something before the challenges his family faced got even more out of hand. The situation could not be allowed to continue. Something had to be done.

Barry splashed water on his face to wash away the tear stains. Then he looked back at the mirror and made himself a promise. "Tomorrow is a new day. Things are going to change. Someone has to do something. Why not me?"

PART 1

THE FOUNDATION

CHAPTER 1

Living in the Truckee Meadows area was a privilege Barry Joseph never took for granted. He loved waking up every day in Pemberton Square; today was no exception. Living in this area had advantages other Reno neighborhoods lacked. Located in northwest Reno, the Square featured modern homes of different styles, definitely not your typical cookie-cutter neighborhood. The neighborhood was neat and clean with mature trees that shaded the streets and houses. Barry loved driving down Mae Anne Lane in the spring, slowing his car to a crawl in order to enjoy the beautiful mixture of pink and violet that colored the cherry blossoms. In the autumn, the colors rivaled the spectacular leaves of New England.

The residents in this fine neighborhood were hard-working and friendly, the kind of people who would give the shirt off his or her back for their neighbor. Everyone kept their yards clean and manicured. Brian Jones lived just down the street from Barry and was the kind of guy who would invite the neighborhood over to watch movies on a bed sheet in the Joneses' backyard and everyone would have popcorn and sodas while Sam McDonald dished up some of his famous homemade ice cream. At Christmas the lights came out, but no one was into the spirit as much as the John Dell family whose nativity scene grew every year. The Dell's twenty-foot trees shone so bright Barry had heard people wondering if the entire Dell residence could be seen from space.

All in all, Pemberton Square was a spectacular-looking neighborhood with a warm and inviting community that made the city of Reno proud.

Until the economy changed.

CHAPTER 2

IN THE DAYS before economic distress hit the nation, there were those who believed in living a modest life, including the Senior Pastor of Bridgepoint Church, Jon Heard. Bridgepoint Church was one of the busiest churches in Reno. The facility offered an elementary and middle school as well as a place of worship. People from all over Reno, especially the northwest area, brought their children to the church schools. The Sunday school in particular was popular due to the straight forward teaching of the Bible.

The thirty-five-year-old church stood at the very peak of the northwest area where its steeple could be seen from miles away. The preaching and the music were outstanding. The church had grown steadily over the years to encompass a 2,000-member congregation.

On a warm spring Sunday in 2006, Barry Joseph sat in a back pew, staring at the pastor intently, trying to understand the message that was being preached and gain inspiration. He leaned back, his leather jacket squeaking against the wooden pew as he absorbed the love of his Lord through the music and messages of the Church. A couple of pews in front of Barry, just off to the right, sat his father, Chuck. His father appeared to be just as engrossed as Barry was.

Pastor Jon Heard stood in front of the congregation and delivered his sermon with authority. His bellowing voice echoed through the rafters. Heard's topic of choice for this Sunday was debt, a very difficult subject to talk about. The pastor's words went straight to Barry's heart.

"You should not have any debt. God does not like you to owe anything. He does not want money to be your master but that only He should be your master. Your head is where your heart is and if you are consumed by what your neighbors have and you try to keep up with the Joneses, then you are a fool.

"God makes it very clear. Just look at Chapter 6, Verses 1-3 in Proverbs. It says the following: 'My son, if you have put up security for your neighbor, if you have shaken hands in pledge for a stranger, you have been trapped by what you said, ensnared by the words of your mouth. So do this, my son, to free yourself, since you have fallen into your neighbor's hands.'"

Pastor Heard looked up from his notes and stared intently around the congregation. "In other words, my dear friends, do not overextend your resources and act in irresponsible ways that could lead to poverty. Be responsible with your money. Do not let your family suffer."

He glanced back at his bible and continued, "Next let's look at Psalm 119, Verse 36 and 37. 'Turn my heart toward your statutes and not toward selfish gain. Turn my eyes away from worthless things; preserve my life according to your word.'"

Again, the pastor looked at the congregation. "So many times money becomes our love. It becomes our God. My wife and I do not have a mortgage. We own our cars. Everything we have is paid for. We owe no one. This allows me to concentrate on God's work."

Barry Joseph looked over at his beautiful wife, Theresa. They'd been married nine wonderful years. He leaned over and whispered in Tess's ear, "Who doesn't have a mortgage?"

"Shhhh." Tess shook her head and frowned.

After the parson had reiterated his point, the service finished with a closing song of "How Great is Our God." Barry stood and followed Tess down the aisle, stopping here and there to visit with someone they knew as the congregation shuffled out of the church. They couldn't linger too long. There was another service scheduled, and the attendees were already starting to file in, just like they did every Sunday morning at Bridgepoint Church.

Barry led Tess through the parking lot and settled in behind the wheel of his beige 2004 Toyota Camry, glad the kids were with Tess's father. He settled into the driver's seat and fastened his seat belt, then looked over at his wife. "Come on, Tess. Who can live without debt? Who can do that?"

Tess tucked a lock of blonde hair behind her ear and shrugged. "Maybe Pastor Jon is good with his money."

"But everyone I know has to make payments to someone."

Tess looked thoughtful. "Maybe we need to concentrate more on paying off what we have. Do you think we live within our means?"

"Maybe not now, but I think it's doable. It's 2006 and things are going great. Our business is fairly steady. People are moving to Reno—some because of the economy, some love the great weather, and some are tired of large fast-paced cities. People from the Bay Area in particular are coming in droves. I can see our economy continuing to grow for some time. Our house is worth well over $400,000, which is amazing considering we bought it for $320,000. Life is good. But getting everything paid off, including the two cars, is going to be quite a task. If we're going to do this, we really need to stick to our budget."

It would be a challenge, Barry knew that. But he had faith they could pull off what felt like the impossible. His father had taught him that hard work and determination could accomplish almost anything. What worked for his father, would work for him, wouldn't it?

CHAPTER 3

1972

BARRY LOVED HIS FATHER. He loved doing every-thing with him from schoolwork to learning about firearm and water safety to helping his father work on cars. He especially loved to play catch with him. Chuck Joseph returned that love a hundred and one percent and couldn't help but notice the gift Barry possessed when it came to baseball. Barry was a natural.

"Step forward with your left leg toward me when throwing, then be sure to follow through with your throw," Chuck said to his seven-year-old son as he demonstrated how to throw a ball.

Barry followed his dad's instructions, his little arm drawing back and then whipping forward in a smooth throw.

"Great job, Son. I am so very proud of you."

"Thank you, Daddy," Barry said with a smile.

Chuck patted his son's shoulder. "My father taught me this when I was younger and now I'm passing it along to you. You'll do the same with your children. It's what fathers do."

"Will I be a father, too?" Barry asked.

"I don't know, Barry. Maybe," Chuck Joseph said. "But when that day comes, it will also bring more responsibilities. You know what responsibilities are, don't you?"

"Like when I take care of the new dog we are going to get to keep Sparky company," Barry said with another smile.

Chuck laughed and ruffled Barry's hair. "Good try, Son. Yes, that would be another responsibility, but no, we're not getting another dog."

CHAPTER 4

1978

"DAD? UH...DAD?"

Chuck Joseph was barely awake. His eyes opened slowly to see his son looking down at him. Chuck's whole body ached from bending over cars and pulling parts at his body shop all day.

He glanced at the clock: 3:32 in the morning. He blinked hard, struggling to wake up. "Huh...? What is it, Son?"

"It's Sparky. He doesn't look so good."

Chuck's chest tightened. Their dog Sparky had been with the family for fifteen years and had been by Barry's side ever since the boy's birth. As far as Chuck was concerned there wasn't a more loyal dog than Sparky.

He could see the worry in his son's eyes, worry that probably mimicked the look in Chuck's own eyes. He'd originally gotten Sparky to keep his wife Betty company while he was working at the body shop, but the lab had worked his way into everyone's hearts. They were all dreading the day brindle-colored Sparky would no longer be with them

Chuck scrambled out of bed and dashed down the hall to Barry's room, his bare feet chill on the hardwood floors. Their sixty-five-pound lab lay on the rug. The dog's breathing was labored. Sparky didn't lift his head, just looked up at Chuck and Barry, distress evident in his dark eyes. Chuck ran for the hall closet, grabbed a blanket, and carefully wrapped the old dog before lifting him in his arms. He turned and found Betty standing in the hall, her eyes dark with worry. They exchanged glances, both knowing but unwilling to admit that Sparky's time on earth was coming to an end.

"Call Doc Malley," Chuck said. "Tell him I'm on my way to the animal clinic. Let me get some pants and a shirt on."

Chuck gently set the dog down on Barry's bed and ran back down the hall. Betty sat beside Sparky, her loyal companion for so many years. With tears in her eyes, she leaned down and kissed the top of his head.

Chuck dashed back into the room wearing jeans and a wrinkled shirt. He gave Betty an anguished look as he lifted Sparky in his arms and ran for the door.

❧

AN HOUR WENT BY. Barry lay in his bed, heart pounding, stomach sick with worry. What was going on with Sparky? When was he coming home?

He was scared. Sparky had always been there for him. When he'd been sick, Sparky would lay in bed next to him. When he was in school, Sparky would sit by the door, waiting for Barry to get home. Mom always said Sparky knew exactly when the bus had dropped Barry off and wouldn't leave the door until Barry walked through it.

Sparky always rode in the car when Barry went with his mom to run errands. The lab loved to hang his head out the window, sniffing the air and wagging his tail as they drove from one place to the other.

He loved to watch Sparky run in and out of creeks and romp through the deep meadow grasses of the Verdi area where they often hiked…

Barry jumped, startled by the sound of the front door closing. He raced down to the front room and stopped, scarcely daring to breathe.

His father stood just inside the door as Betty came to stand next to Barry. Pain shot through Barry's stomach and chest as his father slowly shook his head. Both Barry and Betty ran to Chuck and threw their arms around him. The three stood holding each other for a long, long time.

AFTER A CUP OF COFFEE, Chuck called one of his employees to open up the shop. Then he lit a cigarette and had a second cup of coffee, trying to gather his thoughts. He could hear Betty comforting Barry in his room. Chuck should be in there with both of them, but he needed to get himself together first. He finished his coffee, then headed down the hall.

Chuck entered the small bedroom and studied the walls covered with baseball posters. On his right Steve Garvey stood smiling with a bat on his shoulder, and on his left Brooks Robinson bent over with his glove in position, waiting for a ground ball. Over the bed Reggie Jackson extended the bat as if he was about to hit a baseball.

Barry sat on the edge of his bed, pounding a baseball into his glove. Chuck had to smile. He'd taught his son how to redirect his anger years ago. Better to take his aggression out on a glove than to take it out on someone else.

Chuck sat next to the boy. Barry didn't look at him as he tossed the ball into the glove.

"Son, I'm sorry about Sparky. I know it hurts, but there really is nothing I can say to make you feel better," Chuck said.

Barry dropped the ball, and with his glove in one hand, put his arms around Chuck and started crying again. Chuck held him tight. After a moment Barry let go. He sat back, staring at his glove. "Dad, why did this happen?"

Chuck paused for a moment, trying to find words that would help his son understand. "Poor Sparky's heart just gave out. He was getting old. We already talked about how arthritis was slowing him down. He wasn't the same dog he was five years ago. We all can't be on this earth forever, Son. What you have to remember is all the good times you had with Sparky."

He took a breath, then pointed at one of the posters. "Look at that poster of Brooks Robinson. Brooks retired last year. His life changed and now he has to move on to a different life, a life without baseball. We're in the same position. Our lives have changed. We have to move on to a life without Sparky."

The room was quiet for a long moment. Finally, Barry looked up, his face streaked with tears. "Dad, are there dogs in Heaven?"

"I believe so, Barry. God always has a better plan for us. Keep in mind that Sparky is no longer in pain. He's running around meadows and romping in and out of creeks up in Heaven. But we still have Sparky with us. We always will. He is right here." Chuck pointed to his head. "And he is right here." Chuck pointed to his chest.

Barry nodded and put a hand on his own chest, apparently satisfied with his father's answer.

CHAPTER 5

1979

WHEN HE WAS THIRTEEN Barry helped his father build a storage shed in the backyard. Chuck Joseph laid the plans out on the kitchen counter and they discussed what they were going to do.

"Before we start, we have to get a permit from the city," Chuck said.

"What's that going to cost?" Barry looked at his dad curiously.

"About seventy-five dollars."

Barry didn't understand why his dad had to pay all that money. "But why do we need a permit? We're building it in the backyard. We have fences. The neighbors can't see us. When I talked with Tom Evans about what we were going to do, he said that he and his dad didn't get a permit."

Chuck shook his head. "I don't care, Son. We are not the Evans family. We do things legally here. We do things ethically. We don't try to skirt the system."

"But Dad!" Barry scowled at the plans. He didn't understand, not really. If other people could get away with…

"But nothing. Do you want to pay a fine if you get caught? No, Barry. We do things by the book. Do you understand?"

"Yes, sir." *By the book*, Barry reminded himself, feeling like he'd let his father down though he wasn't quite sure why. *Always by the book.*

CHAPTER 6

LATER THAT SAME YEAR, Barry remembered his father's words. It was a cold January day for the children of Billingshurst Middle School. The skies were clear and blue and the mountains were covered in snow from a snowfall two nights prior.

Jay Lucas was not a bright student. He did not study nor did he care to. For Jay, life was all about fun. Jay hated school, but he liked to intimidate people, using his huge size to his advantage. He was big for a thirteen-year old, already standing just shy of six feet and weighing a hundred and ninety-five pounds, mostly muscle. Both height and weight came in handy when he played football. Made it easy to push people around.

Carl Bowman was a friend of Barry's. In fact, he was one of Barry's best friends. His lack of coordination and his small five-foot, one-hundred-thirty-pound frame made him an easy target for bullies like Jay Lucas. Carl was smart, and in order to survive his thirteenth year of life, he helped with Jay's homework from time to time.

Barry knew what was going on and encouraged Carl to stand up to Jay.

"Why are you allowing him to bully you?" Barry finally asked after Carl had handed Jay last night's homework. He glared at Jay's wide back as the boy shoved through the school's doors.

"Come on, Barry. Isn't it obvious? He could kill me," Carl said, looking at Barry like he'd gone crazy.

Barry didn't care. What was happening to his friend wasn't fair and someone had to do something about it. "You've got to stand up to him," he said as they headed to class.

AFTER SCHOOL, Barry and Carl were walking along the sidewalk on Ambassador Boulevard on their way home when they rounded a corner and saw Jay Lucas standing beside the fence. Carl moaned. "Let's go the other way."

Barry grabbed his friend's arm. "No. This has got to stop."

Carl muttered something under his breath as Barry kept on walking.

Jay waited until they got close, then shoved Carl into Barry and they both went down in the street.

"Hey, shit for brains. I only got a C-plus on that English paper you did for me last night," Jay said.

The boys slowly stood up.

Barry watched as Carl wrapped his arms around his middle, shielding himself from another Jay beating. Carl's face went pale. "I'm sorry, Jay. I didn't want Mrs. Flannigan to know it was me so I put in a few errors and I…"

Barry had had enough. He stepped in front of Carl and glared at Jay. "He won't be doing your work ever again."

"You stay out of this, Joseph, or I'll kick your ass, too. This is between Bowman and me," Jay said.

"No, I won't stay out of this. You know what you are? You're a big fat bully!" Barry said.

"What are you going to do about it, Joseph? Maybe I should have you doing my homework instead of BowWoman here. He seems to be getting pretty stupid lately and you're a smart kid."

Barry *was* smart. He could understand how the things he learned in school would apply later in life. He was going to be a professional baseball player and had realized in second grade there was no reason to hate math. Instead he used math to figure his batting and earned-run averages. He also figured there was no way Jay Lucas was going to stop his bullying unless someone stood up to him.

"The heck I will. You do your own homework, because you're the one with shit for brains," Barry said.

Jay Lucas swung his fist, connecting hard with Barry's right eye. Barry went down hard on the sidewalk, covering the right side of his face as Jay hovered over him.

"You dumb ass! You do what I tell you or you'll get more than a black eye. Tomorrow I have a history paper due on that proclamation by—who the hell was that again?—Lincoln. You better give me that paper before class tomorrow if you want to live, Joseph."

Jay strutted around the corner and disappeared down Hancock Street.

Carl helped Barry up. "Gosh, Barry, that eye looks bad."

"Hurts like heck too." Barry touched his cheek and winced.

"You're going to do his paper, aren't you?" Carl asked.

"I don't know. I got to think that one over." Barry glared at the corner where Jay had disappeared. Standing up to the creep wasn't as easy as he'd thought it would be.

"He'll kill you if you don't," Carl said.

"It seems that way. Cripes, my eye hurts!"

❧

BARRY ARRIVED HOME with his head down. He walked into the kitchen, ignoring his mother as he grabbed a gallon of milk and shut the refrigerator door. He didn't want to talk to his mom, didn't want her fussing and worrying over him. He was furious, more at himself than anything else. And he was scared.

"What happened to your eye?" his mother asked, her forehead wrinkled in worry.

"Nothing, Mom." Barry grabbed a glass from the cupboard and filled it to the brim with milk.

"Nothing! Your eye is going to be black tomorrow. Here, let me get you some ice before it swells anymore."

His mother pulled out a tray of ice and dumped the cubes in a plastic bag. She sealed the bag, then wrapped bag and ice in a flowered dish towel.

"What happened, Barry?" she asked as she handed him the pack.

"Look, Mom. I don't want to talk about it." Barry took the ice pack and the glass of milk to his room.

BARRY HEARD HIS FATHER come through the front door. It was 6:45 p.m. and he was sitting at his desk, working on Jay's paper. Voices murmured downstairs, then footsteps sounded on the stairs. Barry clenched his teeth and turned around when his dad walked into the room.

"Holy cow, Son. Whoever you did battle with got in some good licks. You didn't beat on him, did you? You know violence doesn't solve problems."

"I know, Dad," Barry said He hadn't fought back, but he probably should have. He'd never get rid of Jay now.

"Want to talk about it?" His dad leaned against the door frame and stood there, looking down at Barry in that way that made him feel like a little kid.

"Not really."

"Look, I don't know what happened, but something has to be done. Maybe I should call the school."

"No, Dad. You'll just make things worse."

"Something has to be done," Barry's father repeated, slapping a hand on the desk. "You know how I feel about bullies, and it looks like that's what you're dealing with. Unless you're not telling me the truth about not fighting back."

"I didn't hit anybody," Barry said, staring down at his hands. He'd done things by the book this time—just the way his father taught him. "Pastor Travis tells us all the time that the Bible wants us to turn the other cheek."

His father took a deep breath. "Look, Barry, Pastor Travis is right—you should turn the other cheek, but the Bible doesn't say you have to let someone run you over with a freight train. You're in a tough situation. You can't let this bully get the best of you. You have to fight like a man, an intelligent man. Not with your fists," his dad reached out and tapped Barry's head, "with your head. You might lose, but you have to give it your all. There is no other option."

"With my head?" Barry looked up, frowning. He didn't understand.

"You need to beat this bully — with smarts. You have to come up with something that will make him or her never want to deal with you again."

Barry thought for a moment. A thought popped into his mind. Something that would definitely make Jay never want to mess with him again. Carl either. He nodded and smiled. "Thanks, Dad."

His father smiled back. "Just remember — be careful."

Barry smiled back. "I think I got this, Dad." He got up out of his chair and ran down to the kitchen.

"Mom, I need your help with something!"

THE NEXT DAY Barry handed Carl a box and told him about his plan as they walked to school. Jay was waiting for them at the same corner. "You got my paper done, dipwad?"

Barry grimaced and held out the paper he'd done last night. "Here it is, Jay."

Jay snatched the paper, then looked at Carl. He pointed at the chocolate on the side of Carl's mouth.

"What have we got here, shit for brains?" Jay asked as he grabbed the box from Carl's hands.

"Hey, those are my brownies!" bellowed Carl.

"Wrong, dipshit. They *were* your brownies," Jay said.

"Give it back," Carl screamed.

"You want to live, dumb ass?" Jay asked as he turned and slowly walked away, munching on a brownie.

HISTORY CLASS in Mr. Cane's class was always on edge. The forty-year-old teacher/wrestling coach was tough on his students, but the students excelled because they knew what to expect.

Mr. Cane stood at the front of the room and nodded at the class. "Alright, everyone turn in your papers."

Papers rustled as the students passed their homework toward the front of the room. Jay Lucas proudly handed in the papers that Barry had done for him. "Easy A," Jay said to himself.

THIRTY-FIVE MINUTES into class, Jay could hardly sit still. His stomach felt like someone had blown up a balloon in his guts. He lifted his leg to let out a giant fart, but more came out than just air. Ellen Downing and Gary Turbo both looked at Jay in disgust and quickly put their hands over their mouths. Jay bolted out of his chair and ran toward the classroom door.

"Lucas, where do you think you're...?"

Jay ignored Mr. Cane. His face burned as he ran down the hall, laughter following him from the classroom. He had to get into the bathroom and fast. His stomach was killing him. He wrenched open the bathroom door, shoved into the nearest stall, collapsed on the toilet.

Just as he sat down the stall door blew open with a huge kick. Barry Joseph held the door open, camera in hand.

Jay tried to stand up, to grab the camera from Joseph's hand, but his pants fell down around his ankles, tripping him as he lunged at Joseph.

That's when he noticed Carl Bowman and a bunch of other boys standing in front of the sinks. The boys were all laughing.

"How'd you like my brownies, Jay? You know, the ones you took from me this morning?" Carl asked. He smiled and added, "Or maybe I should say—the Ex-Lax brownies you took from me this morning."

The boys all laughed again, then plugged their noses and filed out of the bathroom.

THE NEXT DAY Mr. Cane handed back their papers. He stopped a moment beside Jay's desk and held Jay's paper just out of his reach. "Mister Lucas, Lincoln did *not* write the Constipation Proclamation."

There was a big F on the front page of the paper.

∾

BARRY AND CARL were called into the principal's office after Jay's parents made a complaint. The boys' parents were called and brought in for a conference. The principal gave a stern lecture about bringing what he called "doctored" food to school, but Barry overheard the principal tell his dad in a low voice that he was glad someone finally had the guts to stand up to the bully.

PART 2

FALLING
APART

CHAPTER 7

IT WAS MARCH of 2008 and winter had worn out its cold bitter blasts. The sun had started to come through the clouds, warming up the northwest Reno area. The warming weather made locals long to garden and wash their cars free of winter grime.

Barry Joseph had grown up in northwest Reno. He had a normal childhood that included skiing on Mount Rose and running cross country at McQueen High School. He'd inherited his father's love of baseball and excelled at the sport, hitting over 400 in both his junior and senior years at McQueen. With the combination of his good grades, athletic speed, and power, he earned a baseball scholarship to the University of Nevada, Reno. During a spring game against Fresno State, Barry took a bad slide into third base, injuring his right knee and putting an end to his playing days.

Barry's big dreams of playing in the major leagues were gone. After two months of disappointment and depression he started drinking. His grades dropped. Luckily Chuck and Betty saw the change in their son. After some serious discussions and a lot of self-examination on Barry's part, he got back on track and completed his studies.

Barry went on to major in business administration. After graduation he worked construction to make ends meet. Construction was hard work. The heat from the Sierra summer sun was excruciating, especially when doing roofing jobs. But the worst job was working a jackhammer to break up concrete. Every muscle in Barry's body hurt after a day on the jackhammer.

One evening after a hard day of roofing, the construction crew went out for drinks at a local bar called Shenanigans. A lovely blond waitress with blue eyes walked up to take the group's order.

"Hi, I'm Tess. Welcome to Shenanigans."

It was love at first sight, at least for Barry. After three years of dating, Tess became Barry's wife. Eventually, the bad knee bothered Barry so much in 2001 he took out a small business loan, quit working construction, and put together his knowledge of construction and business to start Joseph's Hardware.

Seven years later, Barry was making a good living.

He'd expanded his lumber department to keep up with the economic boom and life was looking good.

Until the stock market dropped. Construction came to a dead stop and Barry had to lay off two people, leaving three employees to run the store. The sudden downturn had him wondering just how Joseph's Hardware was going to make it.

Of all the friends Barry had made while he was a student at McQueen High School, Michael Johnson was the best. Michael had made a success of himself in the real estate arena and popped in every now and then to check up on his old buddy. His last visit hadn't been so cheerful. "Hey, Barry, have time for lunch today?"

"I have the time, just don't have the money. What the hell's going on with the local economy?"

"How about going to Jerry's diner on Fifth Street? I'll even buy," Michael said.

"Jerry's closed last week," Barry said.

"Holy crap, I don't believe it. It seems like everything is getting turned upside down."

"You know the Sierra Casino downtown?"

"What about it?"

"Gone. All one hundred and four workers—gone." Barry waited a beat. "And Don's Transmission's and Becky's Donut Hut."

"The Donut Hut too? Ah man, don't tell me..."

"Yep, the Hut's gone too. It's nuts, Michael. It is a struggle out there."

"I know it's getting bad in real estate with all the foreclosures. It's affecting my business," Michael said, staring forlornly at his friend.

"The economy is becoming a mess. You have to hang in there, Michael. We all have to hang in there." Barry slapped his friend on the shoulder and went back to work.

CHAPTER 8

A MONTH AFTER his conversation with Michael, Barry was once again headed to his home on Stone Valley Road in northwest Reno. The wind howled outside, buffeting the car with what felt like thirty-five to forty-mile-an-hour gusts. He was glad he didn't have to drive home through Washoe Valley. He'd heard too many horror stories over the years about semi-trucks and motor homes being blown over.

The news he was hearing about the local economy was all very disturbing. He was already having trouble making ends meet, and experts were projecting the economy was going to get worse? Not good.

Barry drove up Robb Drive past Grace Church and the busy Raley's shopping center where people bustled around putting groceries in their cars. The Starbucks in this center was always busy as well. When he and Tess took their yellow lab, Sierra, out for a walk, he could always smell the coffee several blocks away. He loved having the shopping center so close to home—he could run and get a loaf of bread or a cup of coffee and be back home in a matter of minutes.

He loved the drive home as well. When he drove the Camry, he'd open the moon roof so he could smell the trees covered with cherry-pink blossoms. Enjoying the scenery with the moon roof open was a great way to unwind after a long, hard day at work. Barry wasn't driving the Camry today, but he needed to relax. He rolled down the window and drew in a breath. The state of the local economy wasn't getting any better and neither was his business. He forced his hands to relax on the steering wheel, drew in another deep breath, and tried to count his blessings.

"The economy is out of my control," he told himself as he waited for the stoplight to turn green. "Things will work out. Just do the best you can and be sure to take time to pray. Put it in God's hands. It's all good."

He turned onto Mae Anne and took another deep breath. "Think about your beautiful family; how lucky you are to have their love and support. Think about your beautiful wife and the beauty of the areas around you."

Barry felt the tension ease from his shoulders. Everything was going to be okay. He did some more deep breathing, happy to be heading home to his wonderful family.

He took a right on Stone Valley Road, his tension growing again at the sight of all the For Sale signs. From the looks of several yards, some people had just given up. Usually the Banners kept their yard nice and trim, but now what grass was left was overgrown and full of weeds. An ugly FORECLOSURE - FOR SALE sign sat in the middle of the yard. The same was true of the Murphy's house except their once-green lawn was burnt to a golden yellow because no one was home to turn on the water.

"There by the grace of God go I," Barry said to himself, nervously running a hand through his hair.

He pulled up to his white two-story home, nodding in appreciation of the neatly cropped grass and well-tended flowers. He eased the truck up the short driveway, keeping an eye out for Maggie's tricycle. As he pushed the button on his garage door opener he noticed his daughter's red tricycle on the right side of the two-car garage where he normally parked his work truck. His four-year-old daughter thought parking her red tricycle in Daddy's parking space was fun, but that little trick was rapidly growing old.

"It was cute at first but now it has to stop," Barry said to himself as he opened his truck door, trying not to bang into the Camry. He stalked over to his daughter's trike and yanked it back out of the way, then pulled the truck the rest of the way in and closed the garage door.

At least his nine-year-old son, Daniel, didn't leave toys in the driveway. Barry did have to get on him for throwing baseballs against the garage door to practice his ground balls. Not that Barry didn't understand the need to practice throwing, but the dents in the garage door reminded him that he needed to make more time to spend with his kids. He used to love playing catch with Daniel—it brought back memories of playing catch with his own father—but now playing catch was a luxury that had become increasingly more difficult to afford with the challenging economy. Trying to keep the hardware store running smoothly and at a profit had never been so hard.

Barry let the door slam behind him as he dropped his keys into the tiny wicker basket sitting on the small table just inside the door. His heavy steel-toed work shoes echoed through the house as he stalked across the brown tiles toward the small kitchen. He wove around the short kitchen bar to the refrigerator and grabbed a cold beer. He popped the top and took a long pull of the pale ale. Then he leaned against the counter, staring through the window at the large backyard, a yard big enough to hold the children's swing set and still have enough room for him to play catch with Daniel.

Tess walked in the kitchen without saying a word. He watched his beautiful wife stalk over to the refrigerator and grab a beer.

"Bad day?" he asked.

Sierra dashed into the kitchen, carrying Daniel's baseball glove in her mouth. Daniel raced after the three-year-old lab, screaming at the top of his lungs as he chased Sierra around the table.

"Take it outside," Tess said, opening the patio door to the backyard.

Tess looked over at Barry as Sierra bounded outside followed by Daniel holding a soggy baseball glove. "Guess you can say that."

"You want to talk about it?" Barry asked.

"I don't know. We could be here the rest of the night and there is not enough beer in the fridge to tell you about the whole day!"

Barry grinned. "Why don't you just give me the *Reader's Digest* version?"

He studied Tess as she watched Daniel playing fetch with Sierra. She glanced back at him as if trying to read his mood. "It looks like Maggie has an ear infection again, Daniel needs to sell candy bars for Little League, and my hours at Go Tech have been cut. I'll be working part-time starting Monday."

Barry felt like she'd just punched him in the gut. Yeah, construction was tight and so was real estate, but Go Tech manufactured slot machines. Gaming was one of Reno's most prominent industries and Go Tech was a leading manufacturer of casino slot machines, not only for the Reno/Sparks area, but around the world.

"What?" Barry stammered. "Why?"

"You can blame those games Daniel and his friends play. Our competition is more innovative. Our slots are not as popular as they once were and Go Tech's market share is down. The company just went through a massive layoff. I'm lucky I still have a job."

Barry frowned and took another long pull on his beer. The casino business was a major economic catalyst for the area. If Go Tech was cutting back, that meant even more people were going to be standing in the unemployment lines. He finished his beer and reached in the refrigerator for a second.

No matter how good or bad the hardware store was doing, Tess's job had always been there to help with the finances. Plus her job had provided health benefits for the family. His head started to pound. He slammed the refrigerator door. "Holy shit, Tess! What the hell… We're screwed. You know that, don't you? Totally screwed."

Now was not the time to talk to Tess about the store and its financial issues. Bad enough the store was close to folding. Bad enough the local economy was going to hell in a hand basket. Why did this have to happen now? Why? Barry drained the beer and slammed the bottle down on the counter.

"I know it isn't good," Tess said. She sounded calm, but he could see her hand shake as she lifted her beer and took a sip.

"Christ almighty. Did you get Maggie to the doctor?" He knew it wasn't Tess's fault, could see the pain reflected in her eyes, but he couldn't stop the words pouring out of his mouth.

"Not yet." Her voice broke. "We're already behind on our bills…"

Anxiety made Barry's legs feel weak while anger burned in his belly. He had to stay strong, had to be the fearless leader of his family. And all he wanted to do was collapse on the couch and cry.

"We'll get through this. We have to. Maybe we can get a loan from our bank," Tess said.

Barry stared out the window, the anger in his belly growing. "I talked with them today. They said I'm already overextended because of the store. No way in hell are they going to give me a personal loan."

"Shit." Tess finished her beer, reached in the refrigerator, and pulled out another. Barry frowned. She never drank more than one beer.

"Maybe we can do something about the house payment. I keep hearing about loan modifications. Sounds like maybe the banks are lowering monthly payments in situations like ours." Barry set his empty bottle down beside the first.

Tess nodded and tucked her hair back behind her ear. "Let's look into it. We've been good, loyal customers; I'm sure the bank will work with us."

Barry studied Tess as she opened her second beer. They'd been through some tight times before, back when he was getting the store up and running. He'd found out then just how tough his wife was.

CHAPTER 9

BEFORE SHE BECAME Tess Joseph, Tess was known as Tess Starr of Fallon, Nevada, a small town twenty miles east of Reno. She'd had a rougher childhood than Barry. The oldest of four kids, Tess had to mature fast after her mother died during the birth of her youngest sister, Amy. Her two brothers, Josh and Steven, started working for their father at an early age, helping with the various crops and quarter horses raised on the farm/ranch.

Tess's father, Ron Starr, loved dealing with quarter horses. He was able to sell a number of them to rodeo participants, 4-H kids, and avid riders. The farm portion of the family business was growing corn, soybeans, tomatoes, pumpkins, and raspberries among other crops. Their five hundred and fifty acres produced quite an income for the family.

Until his wife died.

His wife's death hit Ron hard. He ran into financial problems, investing in some grain futures that didn't go well and then losing his shirt gambling at local Fallon and Fernley casinos. He drank to ease his pain and withdrew from life in general. Tess took over her mother's job. She did the cooking and cleaning, and when she got her license, she was their taxi cab driver.

Six years of this took a big toll on the family. Many of the family's close friends saw the strain in the children's faces and pulled Ron aside. They explained what he was doing to his life and that he had a responsibility to his four children. This hit Ron hard. He was bound and determined to change. After this hot confrontation, Ron went to AA and grief counseling. He stopped drinking, but was still behind financially. Finally, he decided to approach his eighteen-year-old daughter for help.

"Tess, money is tight, and I really need your help, Pumpkin."

Tess loved her father. She understood how rough life was without their mom. She was happy her father had given up drinking and was trying to get his life back together. He'd worked hard over the years to provide for them. She could step up and help out.

She found a job working as a waitress at a local café in Fallon. She liked dealing with people—if she didn't count the cheap old men who came in for lunch. But the wages were low and the tips weren't good and Tess felt she could do better. After three years at the cafe she looked to Reno for employment. Not only were the opportunities better, she wanted to go to college. Their financial hardship allowed Tess to apply for a Pell Grant. If she got the grant, she'd be able to take classes at Truckee Meadows Community College on a part-time basis.

A friend of Tess's from the community college told her that an Irish bar in central Reno called Shenanigans was looking for waitresses. She applied and was hired immediately. After starting work at Shenanigans she felt more alive. It was fun seeing the regulars coming in all the time, And Tess loved the sense of community. Her coworkers were her family away from home. If a guy got too drunk or got fresh with her, she would tell the owner, Scott Bell. Scott was an ex-navy seal and didn't put up with anyone abusing his employees. It only took one look at the hulking frame of the six-foot-four man with military tattoos and a shaved head before the offender profusely apologized to Tess.

Tess received her grant. Between work, classes, and the new love in her life—Barry Joseph—she had a full schedule.

After a couple of years Scott sold the bar. Tess had just graduated from Truckee Meadows Community

College with a degree in computer programming and took a position at Go Tech. She then took Barry on as her husband.

CHAPTER 10

BARRY JOSEPH was the loyal son of Chuck and Betty Joseph. He'd always followed his parents' advice, especially his father's. Chuck Joseph was a smart man and well-respected by others. Barry tended to reach out to his father for advice. A week after Tess's cutback, he set out to seek that advice once again. The day dawned, warm and beautiful. The sun sparkled off the white-capped mountains standing tall and majestic against the blue sky.

Barry drove down Sierra Street toward his parents' house on Ambassador. Whether it was the economy or his state of mind, he didn't know, but foreclosure signs were everywhere. He clenched his jaw and focused on the road. "Damn economy."

He passed the Ambassador apartment complex on his right and continued two more blocks before swinging into a long driveway leading to the back of a beige ranch-style house. He climbed out of the car and inhaled, enjoying the sweet scent filling the air. Roses—red and pink and yellow and orange—covered well-manicured bushes. The entire yard looked neat and well-cared for. His father loved to putz around the yard.

"Anybody home?" Barry opened the front door and walked in. His mouth started watering at the tantalizing scent of chocolate chip cookies as he stood for a moment in the small entrance and glanced into the beige-carpeted living room. The TV was tuned into a cable channel, piping Dean Martin music throughout the house. The room still had the fresh smell of the bi-annual paint job Chuck had finished last week. Every two years he painted the entire interior white. Barry raised an eyebrow at the tan wall on the right side of the living room. *Looks like Dad is stepping out of his comfort zone*, he thought.

He walked into the narrow kitchen and wrapped his arms carefully around his mother as she pulled a tray of cookies out of the oven. He knew better than to grab a hot cookie from the tray, but the thought was tempting. Instead he backed away and asked, "Where's Dad?"

"Where he always is—outside in the garage shining up the Caddy again," his mother said, turning around with the tray of hot cookies and setting them down on the yellow granite countertop next to the oven. "Sometimes I think he loves that car more than he loves me."

Barry shook his head. "You know better than that, Mom. He loves you more than life itself. But he loves cars, too. You knew that when you married him. Polishing the old Caddy is how he relaxes."

"On with you now," his mother said. "I'll bring some cookies out after they've cooled."

BARRY FOUND his father rubbing a cloth over the hood of his 1959 Cadillac. He loved to watch Chuck polish the old car. It was like nothing else in the world existed for his father when he was working on the Caddy.

"Hey, Dad. I think you missed a spot."

Chuck glanced up at Barry and grinned. "What's on your mind, Son?"

Barry told him about Tess's hours, the problems with the store, and the bank refusing to give them a loan, then watched his father expectantly.

Chuck picked up a can of car wax and dabbed the cloth into it. Then he rubbed hard at the invisible spot Barry had pointed out. "Well," he said, eyeballing the new wax he'd just spread over the spot. "I can remember eating nothing but beans for months back when I was young. My parents were having a rough time making ends meet. Your mother and I have been through some rough times, too. Thing about those rough times—we always managed to overcome them. Sometimes you just have to tough it out. Things'll get better down the road."

Barry watched Chuck fold the polishing cloth carefully into a small square before swiping the dry side of the cloth over the newly-waxed area. He'd heard his father's stories about the tough times his parents had been through. But the current housing crisis was something his father had never experienced. Maybe a new situation called for a different reaction. "Maybe I could check with the bank to see if they will let me skip a payment or two on my mortgage," Barry said, thinking out loud. "I hear some people are getting modifications on their loans—"

"No!" Chuck turned abruptly and stalked away from the Caddy. He grabbed a clean rag from the neatly-organized shelf and wiped his hands. "I raised you better than that. The Josephs don't weasel out of their obligations. You just need to work harder and smarter."

"I am working as hard as I can now, Dad, and I'm not making it." Barry ran a hand through his hair and slumped dejectedly against the car. "The store is in trouble."

Chuck put the lid on the can of wax, refolded the polishing cloth, and set the cloth on top of the can. Then he put both can and cloth into a small wooden box and slid the box into a space on the shelf. "You might need to get a part-time job or something. God knows, we've all had to do that at one time or another. Maybe Tess can get a second job."

"We're already trying, Dad. I just don't know what we're going to do. We're losing the insurance benefits she's been getting…"

Chuck walked back over to the car, took Barry's arm, and gently pulled him away from the Caddy. Then he used his sleeve to wipe at a spot only he could see. "Son, we are Josephs. We are hard workers and don't rely on handouts."

Barry watched as his father patted the Caddy's hood. Maybe his mother was right. "I'm not looking for a handout, Dad. I'm looking for a helping hand."

Chapter 11

A MONTH HAD GONE BY since the meeting with his father and things were not getting any easier at the hardware store. Barry Joseph didn't see the situation improving at all. In fact, things seemed to be getting worse. He looked into increasing his advertising as well as taking advantage of any co-op dollars he could get his hands on. Most of his vendors would pay fifty percent of his advertising based on the accrued sales of their product. The advertising helped a bit by bringing in some new customers but not enough for the declining revenue. The downed economy bit into his bottom line. Sales had decreased thirty-six percent and the big box stores were killing his business by selling in bulk.

The stress was getting to him. People were scared— *he* was scared. There was no public confidence that things were going to change, but Barry knew something had to change and change quick.

He walked into the living room, noticing the couch, loveseat, and chair framing the brick fireplace as if seeing them for the first time. The oversized pillows placed throughout the room made for an inviting family setting, an atmosphere Tess had worked hard to create. Sierra was in a corner on her dog bed. Tess sat on the forest-green couch reading the newspaper. Tess looked up and slowly lowered the paper into her lap.

Barry dropped down into the comfortable plaid chair across from Tess. Anxiety pulsed through his veins as he nervously ran his hands through his hair and looked over at his beautiful wife. He shook his head, overcome with worry and frustration.

Tess gave him a small smile. "Honey, I know…it is tough out there."

Barry dropped his hands on the arms of the chair. "What's happening, Tess? Where are things going?"

Tess folded the paper on her lap carefully. "We need to look at a loan modification. If we don't do something now, we'll end up in foreclosure."

"You see…" Barry knew she wasn't going to be happy with what he had to say. "There's a problem with getting a modification. When I talked with my dad, he said…"

"Oh crap, you talked with Chuck. I..."

"Now hold on, Tess. Let me at least finish what I was going to say."

"Okay...okay... I'm just nervous. Sorry, but I think I know where this is going." Tess held up her hands.

"As I was saying," Barry continued, irritation making his words sound short and clipped. "We have to hang in there, but how? Dad says we're Josephs and Josephs don't take handouts!"

"Did Chuck offer to help us out? Did he give you a check we can use to pay Maggie's doctor bills?"

Barry's stomach clenched. He squeezed the arms of his chair until his fingers hurt. "No."

"Does your dad have any idea how bad things really are with us?"

"No, not really. At least not in detail." She had a valid point. He just wasn't sure what to do about it.

"Look, Barry. I love your dad. He has a lot of pride and so do you. That's one of the things I love about you. Unfortunately, pride does not pay the bills. We are past the point where we can consider pride. It's time to throw pride out the window. We have to seriously look at doing a modification. Let's talk to Nation One and see what they can do. What do we have to lose?"

CHAPTER 12

IN EARLY AUGUST the weather turned hot. Temperatures registered in the high nineties and low one hundreds for two weeks straight. Reno's Hot August Nights event wound down and life returned to normal. The beautiful antique cars may have left but the poor financial housing situation stayed the same. The sultry heat held no relief—even in the evenings you couldn't sit outside comfortably because there was no air movement. Even though the air was dead calm, the economy of the city was anything but calm. More businesses had closed and very few were starting up. The population was continually decreasing as more and more people sought employment elsewhere.

Tess and Barry's frustration built to the boiling point as they repeatedly called the mortgage company and got nowhere. When they actually got through to a real live person, they were asked to repeat their entire situation over and over again, and when they'd finally explained everything there was to explain, they were often disconnected.

Barry stomach tossed and turned. He could have sworn he was getting an ulcer. Deep inside he not only felt helpless, he was embarrassed about their financial situation. He couldn't figure out how things had gotten this bad. Neither one of them were able to sleep.

The financial strain wasn't helping their marriage. There were times when they would question purchases the other spouse made. Often items were returned shamefully to the stores. The tension even reached the kids at times, especially when asking for money to help in school fund raisers.

One Friday in late August, a letter came from Nation One that said a personal banker in the mortgage department at their local branch, a Mrs. Sue Bennett, could help them. Barry and Tess discussed the issue over the weekend and tried to come up with a plan. They couldn't keep playing phone games. They had to deal with Nation One face to face. So, first thing Monday morning, Barry went to the local Nation One branch on North McCarran Boulevard and asked to meet with Mrs. Bennett. Forty long minutes later, a professionally-dressed, gray-haired woman in her late fifties approached him. "Hello, Mr. Joseph," she said in a friendly voice. "I'm Sue Bennett. How can I help you this morning?"

Barry took a deep breath as a combination of excitement and relief washed over him. He and Tess were finally going to get some help with a loan modification. They were finally going to get their lives back on track. He handed her the letter. "We're having a problem with our mortgage, and I'm hoping you can help us."

Mrs. Bennett glanced at the letter and nodded. "Why don't you come into my office and I'll see what we can do for you." She led him back to a glassed-in office. Barry stepped inside, relaxing a bit as he sank into the comfortable leather chair. Mrs. Bennett's cherry wood desk was neat and clean, holding a single photo of a middle-aged man with a couple of twenty-year olds. Probably her husband and children. Beside the photo were a few awards for her dedicated service to Nation One. Maybe those awards were a sign that he was in the right place to get their situation handled once and for all.

Mrs. Bennett got right to the point. "So, Mr. Joseph, you said you are having problems with your mortgage. What exactly is the trouble?"

Barry cleared his throat and lowered his voice. Bad enough having to talk to a strange woman about his troubles without everyone else in the building listening in. "My wife and I have been trying to get a hold of your company's corporate mortgage department and have gotten nowhere. We call several times a day and we generally get a busy signal. When we finally get through to a real person, that person does not speak enough English to be understood or our call gets disconnected in one of the many transfers. Bottom line is we are having some financial problems right now and would like to discuss modifying our mortgage. We have heard there are several programs available for homeowners in our situation and are anxious to get signed up for one of them." He leaned back and took a deep breath.

Mrs. Bennett sat upright and leaned forward across the desk, handing him back the letter. "Hold on right there, Mr. Joseph. If you've already made contact via phone with our corporate office, I won't be able to help you. I don't want to waste your time. Once you've made contact, any issues that crop up can only be solved in our corporate office. I realize it can be difficult to get through to them, but Nation One has helped a number of people who are having financial troubles. My professional advice is that you keep trying."

Barry's stomach clenched and for a minute he thought he was going to throw up. He couldn't believe he was getting the run-around again. "But what about the letter? It said you could help us. Can't you make a call right now and at least get someone on the line that I can talk to? Your corporate office will answer a call from another Nation One employee, won't they? I really would appreciate that kind of help, you know, just to get us started."

Mrs. Bennett stood quickly and smoothed her navy blue skirt. "I'm sorry. I can't help you. You just have to just keep trying until you get through. That's the only advice I can give you." Then she straightened her shoulders and gave a brisk nod of dismissal.

BARRY WENT OVER and over and over the meeting in his mind on the drive home, his anger building. He slammed on his brakes as a pedestrian in a crosswalk looked up at him, eyes wide. His tires squealed and he slapped his hand against the steering wheel in frustration. The pedestrian, an elderly man with a cane, looked at Barry and yelled, "Hey, watch where you are going, you dumb ass!"

Barry ran a hand through his hair and took a deep breath.

"Sorry!" He waved his hand in embarrassment, then looked at his shaking hands. He'd let the meeting—and his financial problems—get him so riled up he'd almost killed a man!

He kept his mind on the road as he drove the rest of the way home. He tossed his keys in the basket on his way through the door and paused. Tess was talking to someone. "Yes, that is Joseph with a PH, not an F."

He stepped into the living room, raising an eyebrow in question. Tess stood at the window, phone pressed to her ear. Her forehead was creased in a deep frown. Barry could tell she was struggling to keep her composure.

"Can I please get an e-mail address so we can communicate more efficiently?"

Tess grimaced. "What do you mean you don't give out your e-mail addresses? This is the twenty-first century—everyone communicates via e-mail. By the way, where are you located?"

She looked at Barry and shook her head. "Sacraminta? Really? I highly doubt that. I'll bet my right arm you're in India or somewhere close by. You can't even pronounce 'Sacramento' correctly!"

Tess closed her cell phone with a snap and shook her head, her face crumpling in defeat. "Damn bastard hung up on me!"

She folded her arms and shrugged. "I thought I would give Nation One another try, just in case you didn't have any luck at the bank branch. I finally got through to a representative, but it ended up being a warm body located in India who didn't know anything about us or our account or the fact that we have banked with them for eighteen years! Not to mention the fact that neither of us could understand what the other one was saying. I got about as far as a snail on hot pavement!"

Barry plopped down in his favorite chair, reluctant to give Tess his own news. He sighed, lifted both hands, and let them fall back into his lap. "I got nowhere at the branch."

Tess's eyes glistened. Her lips drew tight and he could tell she was trying hard not to cry. He stood and started pacing. "The woman I was supposed to see? The one who was supposed to help us? She said she couldn't do anything because we'd already talked to the main office."

Tess threw up her hands. "Talked to them? How are we supposed to talk to these jerks when they make it impossible for us to get a hold of someone who will actually listen and help?"

Barry flexed his hands, then clenched them into fists. "Michael was telling me how real estate prices have dropped like a lead balloon," he continued. "Most houses in our county are underwater. These are bad times, Tess, really bad times. Michael said his clients are having difficulty getting approved for loans because the appraisals are coming in so low. People are stuck—they can't sell and they can't buy. We're not the only ones in this boat right now. There has to be someone out there who can help us. We just have to find them."

CHAPTER 13

CLOUDS HUGGED THE mountains as the sun rose, coloring the sky in a haze of yellow and white. Chuck Joseph was enjoying a good cigarette with his morning coffee while reading the *Reno Gazette Journal* at the dining room table. He scowled at the picture of graffiti on the new stretch of Highway 395 at the Glendale exit. Darn kids.

"Honey, can you help me?" Betty yelled. Chuck sighed and got up to see what the love of his life wanted now.

Chuck had fallen in love with Betty in high school when he was a guard on the Carson High School basketball team and she was a cheerleader. They married after high school, right before Chuck served a four-year tour overseas in the Navy. Betty held things down at home while he was gone, taking care of the house and a brand-new baby—a son named Barry, Chuck's pride and joy. When Chuck was honorably discharged, the Josephs took up residence in Reno where Chuck made a modest living fixing banged-up cars at the body shop he owned. He loved cars, especially the 1959 Cadillac convertible he'd restored with his own hands. The car stayed in the garage except during the Hot August Nights annual car show every August. He felt like a million bucks when he was driving his pristine red Caddie with his lovely Betty by his side. He loved his car but he loved Betty even more. She was everything to him and he treated her like a queen.

He made the few steps from the dining room into the kitchen, feeling rather spry for a gray-haired, seventy-three-year-old man. He frowned at his wife. Betty stood on a stool, peering into the cupboard.

"I just need the red mixing bowl. It has to be up there, but I can't seem to find it," Betty said.

Chuck did a double take as he noticed the only red mixing bowl they owned sitting on the kitchen counter. *Here we go again*, Chuck thought. *I've got to get her in to see the doctor.*

Up until a year ago, Betty had been able to remember where her car keys were—at an age when most people tended to forget little things like that. But ever since her seventy-first birthday, she'd been forgetting things.

Chuck sniffed at the stench of smoke. He looked at the oven. Sure enough—she'd forgotten the cookies again. The smoke alarm started to scream. Chuck grabbed a towel, pulled the tray of burnt black cookies out of the oven, and quickly walked through the sliding doors out to the back patio. He left the door open as he walked back inside, waving the towel to direct the smoke out the open door.

"Oh, my!" Betty cried as she climbed down from the stool, grabbed a towel, and started waving it frantically. "I'm so sorry, sweetheart. Let me make it up to you. I'll just whip up another batch and then I'll start on that giant birthday cake of yours."

Chuck looked at his wife—so loving, so giving—and fought back the tears burning in his eyes. His birthday was five months ago. He looked into her beautiful green eyes and said, "Tell you what, honey. Why don't you put your baking aside for now and we'll go out for some ice cream at Dairy Queen."

CHAPTER 14

WHILE CHUCK was dealing with Betty, Barry and Tess were dealing with neighbors. They were surrounded by great people. That was one of the best things about living in their community. The neighborhood was full of hard-working quality people. The Joseph's home was two-stories, white with gray trim and a door that matched the blue roof. A white picket fence framed the front lawn. One of Chuck Joseph's best friends, Bob Dugan, lived right next door to Barry and Tess.

The balding, slightly overweight man was a seventy-two-year-old widower. Dugan was outside raking his leaves when Barry took out the trash Monday night. The sun had gone down a half hour ago and heat was fading from the day. Dugan walked over, propped his rake against the fence, and leaned on the rake.

"Hey, Barry. Did your dad tell you we're going fishing on Friday?"

"Bring some back for Tess and I." Barry added the new garbage bag to the others almost filling the waist-high Rubbermaid can and shoved down hard.

"How's business?" Dugan said. "I need to come in and get some carriage bolts for a little project I'm working on."

Barry jammed the lid back on the can and turned, wiping his hands on his jeans. "It's been pretty slow, but by all means, please stop in. I just got a new vendor for the bolts. Heck of a lot cheaper."

He walked over to his side of the fence and put a foot on the wooden crossbar. Wouldn't hurt to take a minute and talk to the old man.

Dugan spoke up before Barry could say anything. "Did you hear that the Wagners were foreclosed on? I can't believe it. I know the economy is bad and people are struggling, but these foreclosures aren't going to help any of us out."

Barry took his foot off the crossbar and stood up straight, suddenly uncomfortable.

"Now we have to worry about our house values going down," Dugan continued. "Just this morning I heard them talking on TV about homeowners asking for modifications, whatever those are. Lazy sons of bitches just looking for a way to get out of paying their bills. Another slap upside the head as far as our home values go." Dugan shook his head and gave a wry grin. "Sorry, Barry. Just letting off some steam. Glad I have people like you and Tess living next to me. God, I hate to think how my tax dollars are helping low-life assholes reduce my home value." He picked up his rake and nodded. "Anyway, say hi to Tess."

"Will do." Barry walked back into his house and slowly closed the door. He placed his right hand against the wall to steady himself and took a deep, calming breath. Dugan was only repeating what a lot of older people, including Barry's dad, were thinking. Hell, he used to think the same way himself. Funny how being on the other side of the fence changed a guy's perspective.

He hadn't seen the trouble coming—nobody had as far as he could tell—but trouble had definitely arrived, and somehow along the way, the people in trouble, the people who most needed a helping hand, were being set up as the bad guys.

Chapter 15

I T WAS A VERY PLEASANT mid-October morning. The weather was getting cooler during the days. Barry and Tess had just finished breakfast, and the scent of fresh toast filled the house. Barry could faintly hear Tess preparing the kids' school lunches. The kids were still asleep and Barry took advantage of the quiet time. He sipped his coffee, concentrating on the Tuesday morning news. He glanced back and forth between the local ABC affiliate, KOLO-TV, and the newspaper's local section. His attention snagged on a TV commercial:

"We can help you keep your home… Thorn & Associates."

Barry was excited. Could there finally be some relief? Would this company really be able to help them save their home? Was there a catch?

He jumped up from the dining room table and rushed to the computer to google Thorn & Associates. When the website popped up on the computer screen, his heart leaped with hope. "Hey, Tess. You've got to come see this!"

His wife came over to the computer, wiping her hands on a towel. "What's all the fuss?"

"This company…right here…," Barry said, pointing at the computer and stumbling over his words. "I think they may be able to help us."

Tess stared at the computer over Barry's shoulder, then hugged him tight and kissed his right cheek. "Damn straight! That's it, honey. This is what we've been looking for. Let's call them."

Chapter 16

A WEEK AND A HALF later, Barry's hope was at an all-time high. The air was cool and the wind was out of the west at thirty-five miles an hour, but the sun was breaking through the clouds, making the air warmer than what the weatherman predicted.

They'd set up a meeting with Gary Thorn and his associate at the Starbucks on North McCarran for ten o'clock in the morning. Barry had done some online research before the meeting. Turned out that Thorn was a very fit thirty-two-year old who'd spent the past seven years in the mortgage industry and had negotiated number of loan modifications.

His associate, Ellen Jackson, had also worked a number of years in finance at a couple of banks. Barry recognized both of them from their pictures online, though Ellen's long brunette hair was more wind-blown from the slight breeze blowing through the Truckee Meadows.

The Josephs walked up to Thorn and Jackson and introduced themselves, then Barry went to the counter for coffee. His hands shook as he grabbed the two cups. This was going to work—it had to. But there was no use letting himself get all worked up. He headed back to the table, handed Tess her coffee, and sat down, keeping his hands wrapped around his cup so no one could see how badly they were shaking.

"So you want a loan modification?" Thorn asked.

Barry couldn't seem to find his voice. He tightened his hands around his cup.

"Yes," Tess finally replied. "We're behind in our payments and have been trying to get through to someone who can help, but most of the time we end up getting a busy signal. If we do get through, the person on the other end is from India and does not speak enough English to be understandable or to understand what we're trying to say. If that's not bad enough, they have the gall to put us on hold."

"How did you end up calling us?" Jackson asked, taking a sip of his coffee and giving Barry an intent look.

Barry cleared his throat twice. "I heard your ad on TV," he said, relieved to hear that his voice sounded normal.

Jackson grabbed a pen, a yellow legal pad, and a form from the black briefcase she had set on the floor. She leaned forward and looked at the couple intently. "I need to know a little about yourselves. You both have jobs, right?"

"Barry owns Joseph's Hardware," Tess said.

"*The* Joseph's Hardware Store?" Thorn asked.

"Yes." Tess nodded. "Business has taken a turn for the worse due to the economy, and I was cut from forty hours to twenty hours a week. Our income has been cut in half and we just can't make the payments. When we first bought the house, we went thru Barge Mortgage who sold our mortgage to Sundown Financial which was bought by Nation One."

"And where do you work, Mrs. Joseph?" Thorn asked, pointing out an area on the form to Jackson.

"Go Tech. We've been going through some cutbacks," Tess said, rolling her cup back and forth, apparently warming her hands from the radiating heat.

"I see," Thorn said, nodding his head. "Nation One is tough to do business with. I've heard this kind of story about them before."

"Can you help?" Barry asked. He rubbed the back of his neck, trying to ease his tension.

"I just helped modify a loan. Took the client's payments from eighteen hundred dollars down to thirteen hundred. Took a few months, but we got there," Jackson replied confidently as she clicked her ballpoint pen.

Hope thrummed in Barry's veins. "How many modifications have you done?"

"We've done a number of them. I would say twenty-five or thirty in the last two months, but these things take time," Thorn said.

"Can you give us some references?" Barry asked.

"Of course." Jackson handed him a folder. "Our brochure is inside along with a sheet of references and the paperwork you'll need to fill out."

"Thanks. What else do you need from us?" Tess asked.

"Well, first we have to have you fill out those forms." She pointed at the folder. "Then we need copies of your utility bills; the past three months pay stubs from you, Tess; profit and loss statements on the hardware store; your last two income tax returns; water bills; any home association statements; and last, but not least, a hardship letter." Jackson leaned back in her seat.

"A hardship letter?" Tess asked, a puzzled look on her face.

"That's right," Thorn said. "Mortgage companies and banks don't just give modifications out willy nilly. They want you to jump through hoops. You have to prove you need it. Then they will go over your expenses.

They haven't started foreclosure procedures on you, have they?"

"No, not yet," Barry said.

"Great. We'll need you to sign a power of attorney," Thorn said. "So we can negotiate on your behalf."

"OK," Barry said after a slight hesitation.

"And if anyone calls—and they will call since you're behind on payments—let them know you are working with us. We have a whole list of connections at each mortgage company or bank that we deal with."

"All right, anything else?" Barry asked.

"Two thousand dollars," Thorn said.

"Two thousand dollars?" Tess gave Barry a worried look. "Do we have to pay it all at once? We don't have that much right now."

"No, you can make payments," Jackson said. She put a reassuring hand on Tess's arm. "We understand that funds are low, but we will need the total two thousand dollars before we send all your information in."

"All right," Tess said. Barry ran a hand through his hair, but he didn't protest. How in the world were they going to come up with two thousand dollars?

The Josephs said they would get back to Thorn and Jackson and headed home.

"At least we have some hope," Tess said as she pulled the Camry door closed and reached for her seatbelt.

"I hope they can pull it off," Barry said.

"So do I, honey," sighed Tess. "So do I."

Barry gave her a quick smile, then started the car. He still wasn't sure where they were going to get the two thousand dollars, but somehow he'd make it happen.

Chapter 17

THE CALLS KEPT coming in and they were not pleasant. A typical call went something like the call Tess received soon after the meeting with Thorn:

"I don't understand, Mrs. Joseph. Why are you behind?" At least the woman on the phone had a southern accent.

"Please refer your questions to Thorn and Associates," Tess replied. "They are working in our behalf."

"I do not have that on record, Mrs. Joseph, and besides, that would be for the modification division. We are the collection division."

"I think you'd better update your records, "Tess said.

"I will do that, Mrs. Joseph. Is there a way you can make a payment today?"

"Look, I just told you we are in the process of doing a modification. The reason we need the modification is because we can't make the payments. And your bank has been inaccessible. That is why we are going through a modification company."

"So that is a no?"

"Yes—that is a no." Tess carefully enunciated every word.

"All right, then. I will make a note of this. Thank you, Mrs. Joseph. Have a nice day."

And so it went.

"Ugh!" screamed Tess as she slammed the phone down for what felt like the millionth time.

"Mommy, are you okay?" Maggie asked.

Tess smiled down at her daughter and tousled her curly blond hair. "I'm okay, sweetie."

Maggie didn't look convinced. "Do you need a hug? When I get upset you always hug me and everything gets better. Do you want a hug, Mommy?"

Tess held her arms out to her beautiful daughter. "Come here, baby, and give Mommy a hug because she really needs it."

Maggie wrapped her arms around Tess's neck. Tess stood with her daughter and held her tight. Some of the frustration eased away as she let tears run down her cheeks.

"Don't cry, Mommy. Everything's going to be okay."

Tess bit her lip until she had her tears under control. "I'll be okay, sweetie. Mommy is just a little overwhelmed. Everything will be okay."

BARRY LOOKED OVER the rail of the upstairs loft, watching his wife and daughter cling to each other. For the umpteenth time, he wished he was a rich man. Goosebumps ran over his skin as a sudden realization struck him. He *was* rich. His family's love was worth more than all the gold in the world.

CHAPTER 18

IT **WAS A COLD** January afternoon. The holidays had left them drained emotionally as well as financially. The store had experienced lower-than-average sales during the holiday season and the collection calls were coming in faster than ever.

Tess was sitting at the dining room table and had just gotten off the phone when Barry walked through the door.

"That's seven times in five days," she growled. She was mad enough to fight a bear, but she wasn't facing bears, she was facing different customer service representatives from the collections department at Nation One. On every single call she'd asked the representative to make a note on their records that the Josephs were working with a modification company. Every single one of them had said they would make a note of the fact. And then she got another call.

Barry went over and wrapped his arms around her. "Another one?"

"Does a bear crap in the woods? Is the Pope Catholic? Are the Kennedys gun shy?" She let her head rest on his shoulder a minute, then pulled away.

"Thorn said we were going to get calls." Barry ran a hand over her hair. She closed her eyes, trying to let his warm touch help her relax.

"I know," Tess murmured. "But I thought we'd be done with most of it by now. How long has it been since we sent Thorn and Associates their two thousand dollars and all the paperwork?"

"Two and a half months, but I have some bad news." Barry let her go and ran a hand through his hair.

"What?" Tess felt her muscles tense up and her stomach knot.

"I got a call from Gary today and he said we need to send him the last three months of pay stubs, bank statements, utility bills, income statements, and so on."

"Shit!" Tess slammed her hand down on the table.

"What did you say, Mommy?" Daniel asked as he walked in the room, his eyes shining.

"I said *shirt*...there was a spot on Daddy's shirt that I was ironing earlier and now I'm telling Daddy about it."

"Okay," Daniel said, but the shine didn't go out of his eyes. "Can I have a cookie?"

"Just one. We'll be eating dinner soon," Tess said as she fished a chocolate chip cookie from the ceramic teddy bear sitting on the kitchen counter.

Daniel grabbed the cookie and raced back to the TV. Couldn't miss his afternoon cartoons, Tess mused. Then she turned back to Barry. "Why the hell do we need to send that stuff again? What happened to all the paperwork we already sent in?"

"They need to update our information," Barry said, grabbing a cookie for himself and putting the lid of the ceramic bear back in place.

"But Barry, your income's changed. The hardware store does more business in the spring than it does in the winter months. Won't that screw things up?"

"I'm not sure." Barry went over to the sink and filled a glass with water. "I hope not. I think this is why they look at the income tax return. Let's hope Gary explains the situation. I'm not sure bank officials understand that some people have income that fluctuates."

Tess leaned against the counter. "That's what I am afraid of. What if they don't understand our situation and base everything on the income statement for April, May, and June—your busiest times of the year. That's not right."

"If they do that, we're screwed," Barry said, turning on the water faucet and filling up his glass again.

Tess stared at Barry and chewed on her lower lip before speaking. "Barry, there's something else."

Barry took a gulp of water and placed the glass down on the kitchen counter. He turned to Tess. "What is it?"

Tess sighed. "Maggie needs ear tubes. I talked with Dr. Shepard today..."

"The ear, nose, and throat guy you took Maggie to?" Barry asked.

"Yes, that's the one. She really has a bad infection. My heart just breaks when she cries from the pain."

Barry looked defeated, nodding in agreement. Tess knew what he was thinking—his daughter was important to him and he would do anything in his power to make her better. She put a hand on his arm. "It's going to cost us big time, Barry. I wish I had better news."

"I know," Barry said, turning his head toward the backyard. Tess followed his gaze, staring at the empty swing and wondering where they were going to get the money.

CHAPTER 19

TWO WEEKS LATER, Tess took the kids to see their grandparents. The warmer weather was melting snow that had fallen the previous night and dense fog was causing heavy traffic on I-80, making travel treacherous. Tess focused on the road, making sure she kept a good distance between her car and the car in front of them. She could feel the excited energy from the kids. They loved going to visit their grandparents.

She breathed a sigh of relief as she finally pulled into Chuck and Betty's driveway. When Tess approached the front porch, she was cheerfully greeted by Betty. Daniel and Maggie quickly ran to their grandmother for a big hug.

Chuck stepped out of the garage, wiping his greasy hands on a mechanic's rag. "Hi, kids," he said with a grin.

"Grandpa!" Maggie and Daniel both ran to their grandfather.

"Hold it right there," Chuck said, holding his hands up above their heads. "I'm a little greasy."

Both kids came to a complete stop.

"Go inside with your grandma," Chuck continued. "She just made some chocolate chip cookies and we need help eating them. I'll join you after I clean up. Then I can give you both a proper hug."

"Cookies!" yelled Daniel with delight.

"Come on, Grandma," Maggie said, grabbing Betty's hand and leading her inside the house.

Tess followed Chuck back into the garage. "Thanks for looking after the kids while I go shopping, Chuck. It's really hard to stay focused on my grocery list when the kids are begging for sugary cereal or candy."

"We love having the kids. They keep us young." Chuck grinned at her as he put his tools away. "Sometimes I learn things from them. Daniel is a whiz on the computer. In fact, I really appreciate his skills in helping me look for parts for the Caddy on the Internet."

Tess grinned back. "I know what you mean. We are so blessed. They both do very well in school."

"I'm not surprised. Barry was the same way when he was their age. Hard to believe how much things have changed. We didn't have computers around when Betty and I were kids."

Tess crossed her arms. "And things keep changing. Just look what's going on around us. The housing market is not good here—it's not good anywhere. Barry said you'd talked about how hard things have gotten."

"Life can be tough at times; you just have to tough it out." Chuck closed his tool box and slid it onto a lower shelf.

Chuck pointed at a box on the floor near the workbench marked "Clean Rags." Tess leaned down, pulled a clean rag from the box, and handed the rag to Chuck. "It isn't that simple, Chuck. We are upside down on our house. We can't believe that we actually owe more money to the bank than our home is worth! We've even hired a specialty firm to help us get a loan modification."

"I can't believe you did that, Tess. We Josephs don't take handouts," Chuck said gruffly.

Tess leaned against the workbench and crossed her arms again. "It's not a handout, Chuck. It is more like a reorganization of your loan."

Chuck tossed the now-dirty rag into another box and turned to Tess. "I believe that when you sign a contract, you abide by it. You don't go back on your word."

Tess held her hands up. "Look, Chuck, I really appreciate your pride and admire the fact that you have passed it down to Barry. It shows up in many ways—good ways. That's just one of the qualities that I love about him. But like you said—times are changing. It's a different world today than it was a year ago. I want my children—your grandchildren—to grow up in a clean, safe neighborhood. I want them to go to a great school. That's why we chose the neighborhood we're in. If we lose the house, we lose the school and everything else along with it. I love and respect you, but I don't agree with you on this."

Chuck winced and rubbed his left shoulder.

Tess frowned. "You see the doctor yet?"

"This is just a muscle twinge." Chuck shrugged and gave her a quick grin. "I have an appointment with Dr. Jorgensen on Friday."

Tess tightened her lips but before she could say anything else about his health, Chuck started talking. "You just have to work with your bank," Chuck said, his jaw set in a stubborn line.

"No, Chuck. You don't understand." Tess paced across the garage and pretended to study the shelves. "That's the problem. The banks won't talk to us. We've tried over and over and over again. The people at the local bank say we have to call their corporate office.

We've called so many times I've got the number on my speed dial. Most of the time, we're connected to someone in India who doesn't even know where Reno is located, let alone understand English." She turned around, raised her hands helplessly, then dropped them again. "It isn't just happening to us. The same problems are going on all across the United States. Nevada just happens to be one of the worst states."

"Why don't you just sell the house?" Chuck asked.

"We talked about that. The problem is we would have to do a short sale and we could still be held responsible for the difference between what the house sells for and what we have left on the principal balance. Our best option is to work with the bank in hopes they will agree to a modification."

"You abide by the signed contract. You just can't just go back and renegotiate. It's something we just don't do," Chuck said, shaking his head and giving her a disappointed look.

Tess threw up her hands. "I understand where you are coming from, Chuck, I really do, but think of it another way. The banks received millions of dollars from the government to help out homeowners in our situation. So where's all that money? In homeowners' hands? No. Just watch the news. Many banks are giving out bonuses to their top executives. In other words, the money is not being used for what it was earmarked for. On another note, if the bank forecloses on us, they'll end up selling the house for less than what they initially got from us. I don't know why this is so difficult for them to understand — they would be better off working with us."

"Wouldn't they get the mortgage insurance money if they foreclose?" Chuck asked.

"Yes, they would. Seems like some kind of insurance fraud to Barry and I, but then again, we're not lawyers," Tess said with a sigh.

"Nor am I. You are in quite a pickle."

"Yes, we are. Please say some prayers for us."

"Will do, little lady. Will do."

Tess gave a quick nod and headed inside to say goodbye to the kids. She swallowed several times to get rid of the lump in her throat. She and Barry had done nothing wrong. They were victims of the rotten economy.

So why did she feel like a little girl who'd been caught with a stolen candy bar?

CHAPTER 20

SIXTY-YEAR-OLD Dr. Bart Jorgenson had worked hard to get where he was. He'd gone to school at the University of Iowa and then worked at St. Joseph's Hospital in Omaha, Nebraska. Jorgenson went on to serve his country, working for ten years as an Army surgeon. After leaving the Army, he opened his own practice and kept that going for the next fifteen years. When he moved to Reno, he went to work at what was then Washoe Medical Center. Washoe Med became Renown Regional Medical Center. He'd been at Renown for over eight years. He loved northern Nevada. The warm weather helped his arthritis and he liked hiking the foothills. He did not like giving patients bad news.

He gave the exam room door a quick knock, then walked in. Chuck Joseph sat in one of the chairs, staring at the posters of the human body hanging on the wall. The big man was alone,

"Good morning, Chuck," Jorgenson started. "I thought you were going to bring Betty with you."

"She's got enough on her mind without worrying about me," Chuck said. "I'm just having some trouble with my breathing. Probably need to cut back on my smoking." A quick smile creased his face.

"I know we've talked about this before, but how long have you been smoking?" Jorgenson asked.

"Since I enlisted in the Navy—right out of high school."

"And you're seventy-three now?"

"Yeah. Look, Doc, I've been doing okay."

"Where's Betty today?" Jorgenson changed the subject.

Chuck shifted in his chair, his face growing red. "She's with her friend Silvia. At the house having some kind of girl gossip session. She doesn't have to…"

"Chuck, your heart has gotten worse. Your blood pressure is high and so is your cholesterol. I don't think what we're doing is taking care of things. We need to change your meds. You really need to quit smoking and start eating better. Cut back on those sweets. It isn't just that you're having a hard time breathing, Chuck. This is serious. We need to do a scan to see exactly what is going on and we need to do it soon."

Chuck stared at Jorgenson. His mouth was moving, but nothing was coming out.

"Would you like me to talk to Betty?" Dr. Jorgenson sat down on the chair next to Chuck. "How about your son? Does Barry know you haven't been feeling well? This is as bad as it gets, Chuck. You need to get the whole family onboard. We can't have you stroking out or having a heart attack. Your lifestyle has to change. Dr. Milborne, the cardiologist, agrees that you need to make some major changes immediately."

Chuck looked down at his hands, a bewildered look on his face. "I can't die, Doc. Betty needs me. Who'll take care of her? You saw her last week. She's starting to forget things and has been very absent-minded lately. She can't be left alone."

Jorgensen put a hand on his patient's shoulder. "You may have to put her in an assisted living facility so you can focus on yourself," he said in a quiet voice. "You need to concentrate on your own health."

"I can't afford that, I can't afford to go through any expensive medical procedures, and I can't leave Betty." The look in Chuck's eyes went directly to Jorgensen's heart.

"What about Barry? Can he help?"

"Barry has a lot going on with the kids, the store, and the house. I'm not going to burden him with my little problems."

"These are not *little* problems, Chuck. And they're not going away. Take on one thing at a time and get things sorted out. You go to the same church I go to. Go see Pastor Travis and…"

Chuck shook his head and glared. "No! I am not some charity case. No one needs to know anything about this and don't you go blabbing to Betty. She has enough on her mind."

"But Chuck, I think…"

Chuck stood and started pacing back and forth in the tiny room. "I said no! I'll get this figured out on my own."

Jorgenson sat back, startled by the reaction from his long-time patient and friend. He'd known Chuck for a long time. They'd golfed together. Their families had gotten together for dinners and celebrations. They even worshiped together in the same church. Betty deserved to know about her husband's condition. Dr. Jorgenson had taken an oath, though. He had to follow his patient's wishes even though he did *not* agree with Chuck's decision.

CHAPTER 21

BARRY HAD BROUGHT Tess and the kids to keep Betty company while Chuck was out. He tried to stay calm while he waited for his dad to get back from the doctor. They were all waiting to enjoy a couple of pizzas they'd ordered. Chuck walked through the door while Betty was busy spoiling her two grandchildren with snicker doodle cookies and listening to them talk about their day. Tess stayed in the kitchen while Barry headed to the living room with his dad.

"How'd it go with old Dr. Bart today?" Barry asked his father as he sat back, enjoying the sounds of family. "Is the old ticker doing okay?" He sipped on the Arnold Palmer his mother had handed him as soon as he'd walked through the door. She always made Arnold Palmers for him when he came and visited, though Barry wasn't quite sure why.

"Not great," replied Chuck, glancing at Barry, then looking away. "He's changing my meds."

"And you still haven't told Mom?" Barry studied the glass in his hands and tried to ignore the burning in his stomach.

"Nope, she has her own problems."

"How *is* she doing?"

His father shrugged. "She has her moments. A week ago I thought she was going to burn the house down."

"Maybe you should think about moving into an assisted living facility," Barry said. He looked his father in the eye. "You need to focus on yourself so you can get better. Someone else can help look after Mom. We have some great places in Sparks and Reno that will look after you, provide three square meals a day, clean your room—"

"This is my home," his father said in a stern voice. "I'm not moving. You grew up here; lots of great memories were made here."

Barry threw up his hands. "But what about Mom? What about her health?"

"She'll be fine. I'm here to take care of her."

Barry respected his father enough not to press the issue anymore. Besides, he wasn't sure where they would get the money for an assisted living facility.

"How is the house situation?" his father asked.

From one tough subject to an even tougher one. He wasn't going to add to his father's worries. Not today. "Things are still rough, but we're working through it."

CHAPTER 22

IT WAS A BEAUTIFUL mid-April Saturday. Flowers and trees bloomed throughout the Reno area. Tess was enjoying an afternoon jog made extra nice because it was Saturday afternoon. Every Saturday Barry took the afternoon off and looked after the kids. As she jogged up to the house she noticed Barry at the door signing for a package from FedEx. She ran up to the door and looked at her husband as the delivery man walked back toward his truck. "What did we get?" Tess asked.

"It's from Nation One."

Tess's stomach clenched. Could this be it? The modification from Nation One?

They went into the kitchen together. Barry took a small paring knife out of the kitchen drawer and slit the package open. He pulled out a stack of paper and looked at her, hope shining in his eyes. Tess squeezed his arm and tried not to yank the paper out of his hand as he flipped quickly through the pages. The light in his eyes faded. He slammed the papers on the kitchen bar and stomped over to the refrigerator. He yanked the door open, grabbed a beer, and popped it open. "We have to make three trial payments of nineteen hundred and fifty dollars each before they'll decide if we even get a modification. Nineteen hundred and fifty dollars. Where are we going to get that kind of money?"

"That can't be right! It should be lower. What are those doorknobs thinking?" Tess said, feeling sick to her stomach as she looked at Barry in disbelief. She picked up the papers and looked them over, her heart sinking with every word. Nineteen hundred and fifty dollars was only one hundred and twenty dollars less than what they were already paying. The language specifying the conditions of the modification made her head spin. The only other thing she could make out was that they had only three days—three days!—to make a decision.

Tess grabbed her cell phone and called Gary Thorn. Thorn picked-up on the third ring. "Hello, this is Gary Thorn."

Tess put her phone on speaker mode.

"Hi, Gary. This is Tess Joseph. I'm here with Barry. We have you on speaker phone. We got a modification package from Nation One."

"That's great news! What did they come up with?"

Tess tried not to scream. "It's only one hundred and twenty dollars less than our current monthly mortgage payment. That's not even close to what it should be based on the financials we submitted to them. The government's program states the modification should be no more than thirty-one percent of our gross income. According to our calculations that's twelve hundred and seventy dollars per month. Plus, it says we have three days to make a decision and *then* they'll decide if we even get the modification."

"We talked about this, remember? I also told you that the amount of the trial payment might not be the amount of your actual payment if and when they do modify."

Tess glanced at Barry. She didn't remember Thorp mentioning anything about trial payments. "How do we know what the actual payments are going to be? We can't afford…" her voice broke and she tried again. "The payments have to be less than that."

"They may be less, or they may be more."

Tess started pacing. "They're giving us only three days to make a decision? That's not very fair."

"And there's nothing in here to clarify how long this agreement would be for if they do agree to a modification," Barry said. "There's no interest rate listed—nothing. It doesn't even say if my principle will be lowered!"

"I told you before—you're not going to get your principle lowered," Thorn said. "Either the past due amounts get placed in the back end or the length of the loan is increased. Yes, they give you a very short time to make a decision. I agree, that can be a bit unsettling."

Barry looked at Tess and frowned.

"But what about our payment being thirty-one percent of our gross income or less?" Tess asked. "All of the government programs mandate that your payment cannot be over that amount. For crying out loud, Gary. This is not what we want. You've got to get in there and fight for us."

"Well, bottom line is that the bank has all the power. You're basically at their mercy," Thorn said.

"That is not an acceptable response. We deserve better than this, this travesty," Tess said. "We paid you to take care of this for us. You have to go back and talk to them. This is very disappointing. They didn't even give us an interest rate."

"I suppose I can appeal the modification if you like." Thorn sounded bored. "However, I have to be honest—appeals have not been very well received."

Barry looked at Tess and she nodded.

"Just do it, Gary," Barry said. "There's no way we can afford this. We have to fight."

"OK, I'll get to it on Monday," Thorn said.

Tess ended the call and looked at Barry, chewing on her lip. "I can't believe this. I thought they had to do the thirty-one percent. If the mortgage companies don't have to follow the mandate, how is anyone getting help? How is the economy going to get better in Nevada? Construction has slowed to a near stop, the real estate market is a mess, unemployment is in the double digits, and I don't see it getting any better. What are we going to do?"

Barry hugged her. "We're doing everything we can, honey. We *will* get through this."

Tess knew he was trying to comfort her, but Gary Thorn's words kept going through her mind: *The bank has the power; you are basically at their mercy.*

CHAPTER 23

FALL WAS BACK and so was football. It was NFL Sunday and Chuck Joseph's house smelled of great food. Every Sunday during the fall Chuck invited his three closest friends to watch NFL football. Each one of his friends was over seventy years old and they'd been friends for over thirty years. This Sunday was special: the San Francisco 49ers against the San Diego Chargers. The Bay Area was just three hours from Reno. A lot of people had moved from the Bay Area to the Truckee Meadows area to get away from the hustle and bustle of the bigger city. Needless to say, the 49ers had a big following in Reno.

"Argh!" The guys screamed as the 49ers lost on the last play with a field goal.

"Can you believe it? They lost again. It looks like rough season," Don Newton said. Newton was a seventy-four-year-old retired Harrah's blackjack dealer sporting his 49er polo shirt.

"You can't force the ball in that kind of coverage. You're just asking for someone to pick it off," Chuck said, pointing at the TV from his recliner. "Heck, my grandson can throw better than this clown. Make better decisions too."

"I can't believe they can just piss the game away like that. Geesh!" Willard Barnes added. Willard was also seventy-four, a former Air Force sergeant who'd spent thirty years serving his country. His son, Brett, had just moved back in with him after losing his job at Donut King and his home to foreclosure. Willard loved his son, but Chuck knew he was happy for the chance to spend time with his old buddies. Willard heaved himself up from his chair. "Well, I better get going."

"I have seven beers left and a half a pan of taco dip with nachos galore. You guys don't have to rush off," Chuck said.

"I'll stay," Bob Dugan said. Bob was a retired UNR science professor and neighbor to Chuck's son Barry.

"With Betty's taco dip just calling my name and some brews? Hell, yes. I'm staying," Willard said, collapsing back into his chair.

"Why thanks, Willard," Betty said as she walked in the room, picked up a couple of empty beer bottles, and took them back through the kitchen out to the recycling bin.

The guys looked at Don, waiting for a response.

"Well?" Chuck asked.

Don peered into the kitchen as Betty headed out the back door. When the back door closed, he sat back in his chair.

"Sure, why the hell not? You jack-offs sure know how to add peer pressure," Don said after a long pause. "But I'll have to text Marge and let her know what's going on."

"You text?" Willard asked.

"You don't? I'll bet your granddaughter would think you were the coolest grandpa if you did," replied Don, spinning a cap off a cold bottle of Flat Tire beer.

"No one says 'cool' anymore," Chuck said. "They say 'you're the bomb'."

"I think they still say cool, but how do you keep up with this shit? Every time I turn on the sports channel, I hear a lot of lingo that I don't understand." Willard shrugged. He dipped a nacho and popped it in his mouth. "This is good stuff. I swear I gain about five pounds every time we show up for a game," he mumbled.

"You bet your ass it's good. Betty has a secret recipe," Chuck said.

"Yeah and that's where the five pounds go every time—right to your fat ass," Don said.

Everybody laughed.

Betty came in with a covered bowl and handed it to Willard. "Here you go, Willard," she said with a smile.

"What's this?" Willard asked.

"It's my taco dip, silly. I know how much you like it, so I dished some up for you to take home."

"Wow! That's awfully nice of you! Thank you, Betty." Willard took the bowl with a smile.

Betty smiled back and gave Willard's hand a friendly pat. "It's not all for you, now. Share some with Mary."

Willard looked curiously at Chuck and then at the rest of the guys.

Betty waited, smiling.

"But, Mary passed a…" Willard started.

"I think Betty was trying to say that she wants you to share it with Brett at home," Don interrupted. Chuck gave him a grateful look. Don always seemed to catch on the fastest.

"Oh, ah…thank you, Betty," Willard said. Betty nodded and headed back to the kitchen. Willard gave Chuck a puzzled look, silently asking for an explanation.

"Look, you guys have another beer and enjoy some game highlights while I help Betty in the kitchen," Chuck said, climbing to his feet. "There's some beer left—"

"What the hell is going on here, Chuck? We've all been friends for years. We do things together, we share vacations together. Is there something you need to tell us?" Bob asked, his right eyebrow lifted in question.

"Yeah, Chuck. What gives? What's happening to Betty? She was at the funeral. She knows Mary died," Willard said.

Chuck stopped before entering the kitchen and turned around, facing his friends.

"I know, I know, and so does Betty," Chuck said, tears in his eyes.

His friends just stared at him.

"At times...," Chuck said, hesitant to talk about what to him was a very sensitive subject but not knowing what else to do.

"Well," Bob finally said as the silence drew on.

"Betty has Alzheimer's." Chuck thought he would choke on the words.

"Hey, buddy. Is there something we can do?" Don asked. He walked over and put a hand on Chuck's shoulder.

Chuck shook his head. "No, I'm taking care of her. She just gets confused at times."

"Well, she's a lovely woman and treats us all like kings when we come around," Willard said. "It's a good thing you're here to take care of her."

"Ah, yeah...sure...," Chuck said. *I'll be here, but for how long?* he wondered.

Chapter 24

MICHAEL JOHNSON strolled into Joseph's Hardware feeling kind of down. The economy had taken its toll on the real estate market and being a realtor these days in Northern Nevada was not nearly as lucrative as it had been a couple of years back.

Michael was tired and depressed. He'd never imagined his life would be a mess at this age. He had a few hours to kill and he wanted to see Barry. Maybe talking with his old friend would help his mood.

The six-foot-two, two-hundred-pound Johnson was just not himself these days. He was exhausted from working two jobs trying to make ends meet. In addition to working real estate during the day, he'd taken on a part-time job as a night watchman at the Ralston Purina facility in east Reno. He often wondered if he should just quit the real estate business altogether like a lot of agents had and move to a place where the economy was better.

"You look like shit, old buddy. Burning the candle at both ends?" Barry asked.

Michael watched him use a utility knife to open up a box of calking guns. He shrugged. Of course he looked like shit. No need to take it out on Barry, though. Guy had enough of his own problems. "Working two jobs has been rough."

"Just sell a couple of houses and you can quit the Barney Fife job at Ralston," Barry said, placing the guns carefully on the manufacturer's display shelf.

"It's not that easy, Barry. When I do finally get a sale, it's either a foreclosure or a short sale. When that happens, I have to wait for the bank to approve the sale. And those banks always want to get the maximum out of each property. In fact, right now I have seven homes in escrow and they're all short sales. So, I'm sitting here, waiting for the big banks to make up their minds. On the other hand, my buyers are anxious and are getting impatient. They want me to show them a regular house for sale and not a financially distressed house because they want to move in now. The problem is that there are not many homes in inventory that are not in distress."

"Wow, that really sucks, Mike." Barry set the last gun on the display and headed back to the counter. Michael followed him.

"Agreed! Plus, it seems like more folks are moving out of their homes and then renting them out. That doesn't help me. It helps the property management folks, but not me." Life was tough all the way around, Michael realized. Both for those who had jobs and those who needed them.

Chapter 25

Somehow time passed and once again it was late April, seventy degrees and sunny in the Truckee Meadows. Tess entered the office of Great Basin Gaming, filled with hopeful excitement. The pleasant office was in a two-story building on Longley Lane in east Reno. The heavy glass door to the Director of Operations' office had the name *Miriam Grant* printed on a brass plate. Tess was right on time for her two o'clock appointment.

Miriam Grant was a fifty-three-year-old woman with graying hair. Loyal and hardworking, Grant had started out on the production line. The people at Great Basin Gaming had seen her potential and promoted her until she had reached her current position. Tess had checked the woman out online and had been impressed. Now she waited in anticipation. This was her third interview for the project manager position offered by the company.

"Have a seat, Tess," Grant said.

Tess took a seat in front of Grant's metal desk and smoothed the skirt of her cobalt-blue dress. Her excitement grew as Grant went over the job description in more detail than she had in their previous meetings. When Grant started telling her about the company's benefits, Tess had a hard time keeping the smile from her face. Maybe this time…

"Well, Tess. We are impressed by your past work experience at Go Tech and your references are glowing. How would you like to work for us?" Grant asked.

"Yes…Yes…!" Tess said, feeling like any minute she would rise up into the air and float around the room like an inflated balloon. "I would love to!"

"Great! You can probably start in a week."

"Awesome."

"We'll need you to take a drug test today, and we have a couple of other things look at. Then I'll give you a call and give you an exact starting date," Grant said.

"Thank you, Ms. Grant."

"Just call me Miriam. It looks like you'll be working with us very soon."

"Thank you, Miriam."

Tess left full of hope. Finally, something good was happening. It was about time!

CHAPTER 26

M AY ROLLED IN wet and stormy. The temperature dropped on the valley floor as dark clouds oozed over the mountains. Rain pounded northwest Reno. Barry and Tess's roof couldn't take the pounding. The twenty-one-year-old roof had gradually lost its wooden shingles to repeated pigeon stomping, holiday decorating, freezing snow, and driving rain. The storm tore off another shingle and rain ran into the new hole. The water dripped through the insulation and spread across the ceiling, slowly seeping through the gypboard to fall to the bedroom carpet with a steady drip, drip, drip.

"Oh, crap!" Barry jumped out of bed.

"What the heck is going on?" Tess said, not happy at being woken up at three in the morning.

"We've got a leak," Barry said, turning on a light before running to get a towel.

One more thing to stress out about. Tess got up with a groan and ran to get a bucket. As she was going down the stairs she stepped on another wet spot in the carpet. She stopped and looked up at another leak. "Shit! We've got another one in here."

After setting out buckets and laying down towels, the couple tried to go back to sleep. They both lay quiet, listening to the constant plop, plop, plop.

"You know we are going to have to replace the roof," Tess said.

"We can't afford that right now." Barry rolled over on his side and faced Tess. "Besides, what if the bank forecloses on us? Why would we want to put money into this place when we might not even be here the next time it rains?"

"We can't keep living like this." Tess buried her face in her pillow for a moment, then flopped over onto her back in frustration. "I pray the appeal goes through so we can finally put this damn mortgage problem behind us."

"We can't count on that." Barry flopped over on his back. "We've got to face it, Tess. We may have to move."

"What about the roof?" Tess asked quietly. She couldn't believe Barry was ready to give up.

"Right now, the roof is the least of our problems."

CHAPTER 27

TWO DAYS LATER, the rain continued to soak the valley floor, adding volume to the melting snow flowing off the mountains. Many of the streets in the area flooded. All the water was great for the early summer months but not for the Joseph's roof. Buckets and pans sat scattered across the floor in an attempt to keep up with the leaks.

Tess was up before everyone else. Barry was still sleeping after a long night spent working on the store's books. He'd asked his assistant to open up the store.

Tess's cell phone rang. They'd gotten rid of their land line several months earlier in an effort to cut back on their monthly expenses. Losing the land line hadn't been hard—everyone always called Barry and Tess on their cell phones anyway. Tess recognized the number. Her heart pounded in her chest. She took a deep breath, pushed the answer button, and held the phone to her ear. "Hello, this is Tess."

"Tess, this is Miriam Grant from Great Basin Gaming. Are you free to talk?"

Tess felt giddy. This was what she'd been waiting for. Now life could get back to a financially healthy normal.

"Absolutely. What's up?" Tess asked with a smile.

Miriam's voice was cooler than it had been during their last interview. "We've gone over your background check and found a problem. Well, actually, it is your credit."

"My credit?" Tess couldn't believe what she was hearing. She ran her free hand through her hair. Excited anticipation turned into anxious worry. Her stomach rolled.

"Yes, your credit. I'm sorry, Tess, but I can't give you the position," Grant said.

"But what does my credit have to do with this?"

"Company policy." Miriam Grant's voice softened. "I'm so sorry, Tess. Good luck with your job search."

Tess stared at the phone for a long time after Grant ended the call. What had just happened? She slowly closed her eyes and tilted her head back, pausing for a long moment. When she opened her eyes, she found herself staring at one of the four wet spots in the ceiling.

Her eyes welled with tears. She didn't know whether she was more frustrated or depressed. She pounded her fist on the counter top.

Just then Barry walked into the kitchen. He opened the cupboard. Tess tried to stifle a sob, but he noticed.

"Honey, what's wrong?" Barry asked.

Tess quickly grabbed a couple of tissues, then shoved the tissue box back on the counter. She took several deep breaths, trying to gather herself emotionally. This was not going to be easy. After all they'd been through, the job with Great Basin Gaming was supposed to be the break they needed. She swallowed hard. "That was Miriam Grant. I didn't get the job."

Barry stared at her. "I thought it was in the bag. What happened?"

"Seems it's company policy to run a credit check on potential employees and…"

"And they found out our credit is bad and because of that you didn't get the job."

"Yeah," Tess wrapped her arms around her waist.

Barry leaned back against the counter and folded his arms. "When it rains it pours, honey. We'll get through this. Don't ask me how, but we will."

How could he be so nonchalant? "I don't know if I can take any more. I feel like the world just threw me down and ran a marathon over me," Tess said. She stared at the kitchen floor, feeling as low as the pans they'd set out to catch the drips.

"Look at me."

She couldn't bring herself to look up. She'd let her husband down. She'd let everyone down...

"Tess. Look at me."

Finally, Tess looked up, her vision blurred from her tears. Barry touched her cheek tenderly and the tears started to fall.

"Tess, we'll get through this. This is war; we have to keep fighting. We have gotten this far, and if we cave in now, Nation One wins. Do you want them to win?"

"No."

Tess clung to his warmth as Barry wrapped his arms around her. "Honey," he said in a low voice. "I love you. We'll get through this and one day we'll look back at this as the biggest battle we had to face. The day will come when we'll get through to the right person at Nation One. As for the new job—evidently the good Lord did not intend for you to have it. Personally, I think the folks at Great Basin made a mistake. It's a bad policy that led to a dumb decision. How do they expect to find someone who meets their criteria? Hardly anyone has great credit right now."

Barry looked down at her. "We'll be stronger when this is all done. Remember, the most important thing is that we have each other."

He was right, Tess knew that. They would get through this mess, one way or another. She couldn't help but wonder how many more challenges they would have to face before they finally reached the other side.

CHAPTER 28

DRIVING EASTBOUND from Verdi to Sparks on I-80 always had its challenges. Many California motorists came across the border going eighty miles per hour or more, making them easy prey for the Nevada Highway Patrol. Many Nevadans turned a cold shoulder to the California drivers because of their offensive driving style. Even though Reno was a vacation destination, and the locals appreciated the influx of dollars, the reckless driving created an irritation for working folks on their way to the office. California drivers almost always seemed confused driving around the area, a fact that drove many Nevada drivers nuts. One of the worst areas to navigate was the I-80 and Highway 395 inter-change, an area better known as the Spaghetti Bowl.

Barry was one of the locals taking the Highway 395 North exit after a great lunch at the Peppermill buffet — paid for by one of his vendors. They'd been discussing how he could buy his products in bulk with other local non-competing hardware stores, a move that would give him the same price advantage as big box stores. He'd just entered the two-lane curve leading to I-80 when an eighteen-wheeler flew by him on the right side and started to move into Barry's lane. Barry stepped on the brakes, trying to move his Chevy pickup as far left as he could. His front fender scraped against the guardrail. The sound of shredding metal echoed in the underpass as his truck dragged to a stop. The semi was long gone. It was either on its way to the north valleys or had taken one of the many exits along the way.

The front left side of the pickup was in pieces thanks to the sharp guardrail. Bits of fiberglass and metal littered the freeway behind him. He cursed as cars rushed by. Then he pulled out his cell phone and called for help. Barry was told an officer was on the way, but it was a little late for the highway patrol. He hadn't even gotten the license number of the truck. All he remembered was a red cab with a silver cargo box and California plates. That could be almost any eighteen-wheeler on the road. He leaned against the guardrail and called Tess. She was calmer about the accident than he'd expected. They had insurance after all, she reminded him, and he wasn't hurt. But there was the matter of the deductible…

"So, you have the policy in front of you, Tess?"

"Yes, I told you, it clearly states a one thousand dollar deductible."

"Ah, man!" Barry slapped the guardrail. "I thought it was five hundred dollars. What happened to our five hundred dollar deductible?"

"We had to increase our deductible to a thousand dollars in order to get our premium down, remember? We discussed this months ago, and you told me to go ahead and make the change with our insurance company."

"I don't remember, but it doesn't matter." Barry sighed. "Bottom line is that we can't afford this right now. The bills are piling up. When it rains it pours, and our financial situation is becoming a friggin' monsoon. Damn it!" Barry held the phone away from his face so he didn't scream in Tess's ear.

He glared at the trooper who'd just pulled up. The trooper would assess the damage and write up a report, but who was going to pay the deductible?

CHAPTER 29

SUMMER PASSED in a blur and the Joseph's financial situation kept going downhill. Tess tried not to think about it all the time, especially at times like this, when she and Sierra were out for their evening walk. The September sky was spectacular as the Nevada skies can sometimes be, the purples and reds running together in the east in a breathtaking display. The view always amazed visitors and locals alike. As far as Tess was concerned, there was nothing in the country like Nevada sunsets.

Dusk was Tess's favorite time of day. She loved the silhouetted mountains and the sky that looked like an artist had painted the clouds, leaving brush marks where the winds moved them.

It was almost dark. Sierra walked obediently beside Tess. The O'Brien's German shepherd barked but Sierra and Tess kept moving as if nothing had happened. Sierra was doing beautifully. Both Tess and Barry had worked with her for hours when she was a puppy, their training guided by their friend who owned Scraps, a local pet store. The hours spent training made their evening walks a pleasant stroll instead of the tug-o'-war they'd had before all the training.

On their way home, Tess saw a man she didn't recognize sitting on the front steps of the old Meyer home, a home that had been recently foreclosed on. As she walked by the old white split-level house she acknowledged the man with a nod. "Nice evening."

The grubby fortyish-looking man said, "Yes, it is." He got up without saying anything more and went inside the dark house.

The foreclosure notice was still displayed in the window.

Puzzled, Tess took Sierra around the block one more time. The house was still dark, except for what looked like a small candle burning inside. Tess went up about three houses and called out to her old friend, Julie Johnson, Michael Johnson's wife. "Hey, Jules! Who's the new guy in the old Meyer house?"

"Good question. Michael said the house hadn't been bought up."

"What?" Tess frowned. "Then who *was* that guy?"

"That, my friend," Julie said with a frown, "is what we call a squatter."

CHAPTER 30

WHERE SEPTEMBER had been warm and sunny, October rolled in with a bang, declaring summer was over and winter was on the way. Clouds hung low over the valley, lending a dreary feeling to the day. Once again rain poured down so hard and fast the street gutters backed up. Water rose in the streets and splashed onto the sidewalks, drenching anyone walking by. The front door clanged at Joseph's Hardware and Barry looked up to see Michael Johnson enter the store. Michael wove his way past the heating filters, calking guns, and rakes to the front counter. Barry set down the inventory sheet he'd been going over. He had some tough decisions to make. Somehow he had to save more money. Maybe he should just sell the inventory he had on hand and not reorder certain products. Or he could go cheaper on other products. He scowled. He'd rather just reorder everything but the economy was still too slow. He looked up at his dripping wet friend.

"Hey, Mike. You scuba dive to get here or what?" Barry grinned.

"It's really coming down out there. It's ruining this suit." Michael swiped rain off his pants. "Got any umbrellas?"

"This is a hardware store, not a Target." Barry went into the adjoining back room, grabbed his old umbrella, and brought it out to Michael. "Here, take this. I don't have to wear a suit every day like some corporate big shot."

"Thanks, Barry. I appreciate it. Are you going to be okay without it?" Michael said, taking the umbrella with a rueful grin.

"I'll be fine. I parked right next to the door in the back alley and it has an overhang, so I should stay dry." He thought for a moment. "But get it back to me. Tess's father gave that umbrella to me as a gift."

Michael was looking at the handle of the umbrella, trying to figure out how it opened. He evidently found the right button as the umbrella started to unfold. Michael clicked the umbrella closed again and nodded. "No problem. I'll get it back to you."

"What's going on in the real estate market?" Barry asked.

"You got all day?" Michael asked, shaking his head with a frown.

Barry looked at him in disbelief. How could things get worse? "Come on, Mike. It can't be all that bad."

Michael shot him a look. "Oh, yeah? Here's just a bit of what's going on. I already told you that over sixty percent of the homes for sale are distressed homes, but do you know what is going on with the foreclosed homes?"

"What?" Barry asked, not really sure he wanted to know the answer.

"For starters, I was inspecting a house the other day and the whole thing was stripped."

Barry shrugged. "That doesn't sound so bad. A lot of people take the curtains or blinds."

"No, you don't understand. These guys are pulling up the carpet, ripping the sheet rock off the walls, and taking the electrical covers and outlets as well."

Barry stared at his friend, mouth open in shock. "You can't be serious."

"And get this—Cindy from our office looked at a house yesterday and someone had poured cement in the toilet," Michael added.

Barry shook his head. "What are people thinking?"

"They're not thinking, they're just mad. Old Gene was going to put a house on the market until he inspected the pool in the backyard. It was covered with moss and mildew. The people who owned the place had just let it go. There were even mosquitoes out there, buzzing around like crazy," Michael said.

"Holy cow."

"That's not everything."

"There's more?" Barry asked, surprised.

Michael grabbed a small wrapped peppermint from the bowl Barry kept on his counter and put the candy in his pocket.

"Oh yes. We've been working a lot with the Humane Society because people have been leaving their pets behind."

"That's horrible. Is it hard to sell these homes?"

"Not so much—if the freakin' banks will work with you."

"The freakin' banks." Barry sighed, shaking his head. It always came back to the banks.

CHAPTER 31

THE END OF OCTOBER turned warm again. Thursday morning dawned sunny and the temperature rapidly rose into the seventies. Michael was taking a real estate client on a tour of the Hidden Valley area. He climbed into his 2007 olive Subaru Outback, excited about the opportunity for a big real estate score. Joel King—*the* Joel King—a big real estate investor, slid into the passenger seat. King was interested in taking advantage of the low interest rates and the abundance of available homes.

"The last couple of homes were pretty good, Mike. I hope we can keep this up."

"I think so." Michael looked over his shoulder as he backed out of the driveway. "It's too bad we have this many homes to choose from, too many foreclosures and short sales."

"Hey, some of these deadbeats got in over their heads. I love it. They shouldn't have bought those houses in the first place. The market was way over-priced. But hey, this is just the way I like it. The King is here and he is going to build his own little kingdom right here in Reno Friggin' Nevada."

Michael tamped down his rising anger and changed the subject. "At one time we had over two thousand people a month moving into the area because economy was so good and the housing prices were booming and—"

"Hey, Mike. See that beautiful home over there?" King nodded out the window.

"That huge thing on the hill?" Michael asked, pointing at a home with yellow stucco siding and a clay tile roof as they drove past Rattle Snake Mountain off McCarran.

"Yeah. I want to buy it."

"But it's not for sale, Joel."

"It will be. I bet the owner's like all the other dead-beats in this one-horse town. He's probably upside down right now and almost ready to dump it. He is probably trying to sweat it out. Let me know when he dumps it. I want that home," King said, looking at his nails and pushing back a cuticle.

Michael had had about enough of this blowhard. Didn't the guy realize he was making fun of Michael's hometown? It was more than irritating. He'd had to spend all day yesterday listening to how great this guy was even though he'd inherited everything. Probably never worked a hard labor job in his life. Instead of selling him a house, Michael wanted to deck this joker.

Michael pulled into a 7-Eleven. He couldn't afford to blow a possible sale, still… "Excuse me, Joel. I'll be right back."

Michael ran inside the bathroom. He went up to the nearest sink and looked down at his shaking hands. He took a few deep breaths, trying to calm his nerves. Then he turned on a faucet and splashed water on his face. He glanced in the mirror as he patted his face dry. "How can you put up with these greedy, heartless bastards?" he asked his reflection.

His reflection didn't answer.

CHAPTER 32

YEAH, REAL ESTATE business was bad, but the roofing business was worse, at least as far as Harold Frank was concerned. He'd been in the roofing business for over seventeen years. He'd started out with a crew of four and worked with as many as five crews when the economy was good. Now he was down to two employees, one a part-timer. Projects were few and far between. He'd been slashing his prices to try and keep ahead of the competition and had to basically reinvent himself, specializing in remodels instead of new homes.

Frank had been a customer at Joseph's Hardware ever since the store opened, and he loved the opportunity to work for the Josephs. But he hated being the bearer of bad news. The Joseph roof was bad. Real bad.

After stepping down from the last rung of the ladder, Frank gave Barry a long look. "How long has it been like this?"

"I would say about two years now."

Frank wasn't surprised. Seemed roof maintenance was low on everyone's list these days. "I won't kid you, Barry. You need a new roof. That plastic tarp you tacked up there isn't cutting it. Not only is the tarp torn, the wooden shakes are coming loose underneath it, and the exposed felt is torn so bad that I can see the plywood sheathing."

Barry shrugged, looking faintly embarrassed. "I know, Harold. Things have been tough. I put the plastic tarp up hoping it would get us by until business picks up. Looks like hell, doesn't it?"

Frank laughed. "Yeah, it looks like shit."

Barry's face went red. He chuckled, but Frank didn't know whether it was from amusement or embarrassment. "So what's the bad news?"

"Well—if you would like me to do the whole roof…" Frank scratched his head and squinted up at the roof. "That would mean replacing any rotten plywood and laying down new felt and replacing your wooded shakes with asphalt shingles. For the whole roof, I'd have to charge you nine thousand six hundred dollars."

He watched as Barry kicked at the dirt. He looked back up at Frank. "Look, I can't afford that right now. I'm struggling to keep my head above water. Can you do some kind of patch job?"

Frank studied Barry for a long moment. He took a deep breath and gave a quick nod. He'd known Barry for a long time and the guy always gave him some kind of break when Frank went in the hardware store. "I can probably do something for around a thousand dollars. I'll need to replace some wooden shakes and a sheet of plywood here and there."

"I can get you plywood and nails and anything else you need from the hardware store."

Frank nodded. "I know that, Barry. I'm counting on it."

Barry looked at him, eyes wide. "You mean you figured that into your estimate?"

Frank looked at Barry's glistening eyes and shrugged. "Look, I've known you for what…oh, hell. It's been a long time. I'll do the best I can." He looked back at the roof to give the other man a chance to get himself back together.

"Can you give me a week to get the money together?" Barry's voice sounded muffled.

"I can do that. I have some other work anyway. I'll go back up and get together a list of materials you can get for me," Frank glanced back at Barry. "It'll cost you a beer or two when I'm done."

Barry was grinning from ear to ear. He looked Frank in the eye and said, "Crap, Harold. You drive a hard bargain."

Frank just smiled and shook his head. He wasn't going to make any money on this deal, but what the heck. "Yeah, I'm a real bad ass."

Chapter 33

Barry had to get the roof fixed before winter set in for good. Harold Frank had offered him a good deal, but he still had to figure out where to get the money.

He'd always had a great relationship with his father. Chuck had always taught Barry right from wrong, lessons Barry hadn't always appreciated at the time. He remembered when he was eight years old and his father made him go back into the local grocery store to apologize to the manager for stealing a candy bar.

Today Barry felt like that eight-year-old boy again. He was going to approach his father and ask him for money. Something he never had done before.

Chuck was sweeping out the garage when Barry drove up in his pickup. He leaned the broom against the garage door frame and walked up to the car. "What are you doing here?"

"I came to see you." Barry was a bit surprised by the question.

"Everything okay?" Chuck had a funny look on his face.

Barry glanced over his father's shoulder. "Not really. Actually everything is getting more frustrating. Is Mom okay?"

"Your mother is fine. Are Tess and the kids okay?"

"Yeah, they're okay," Barry said. He glanced around—something was different. He chose to ignore his feelings for the moment. "Look, Dad. I really need your help. My roof is leaking and I can't afford to get it fixed. We're down to our last few bucks in the savings account and I don't know what to do. I can't borrow off the house and I already maxed out my credit on the store so—"

Chuck cut in with a quick wave of his hand. "You're hoping I can help you out?"

"Well…yeah…" Barry stammered. He glanced at the neatly trimmed rosebush at the side of the driveway. "I'm sorry to bring my problems to you, Dad, but—"

"How much do you need, Son?"

Barry looked back at his father in surprise. "What?"

"How much do you need?" Chuck repeated. Barry tried to read his father's face, but couldn't tell what was going on inside the man's head.

"It'll cost just about a thousand dollars to patch up my roof. I'd like to have Harold Frank make the repairs. I just don't have time, I'm already putting everything I have into keeping the store running. Heck, Dad. I'm at my wits end. I just want..." Barry hesitated, fighting the tears burning in his eyes.

"Hold on." Chuck went into the house. Barry swallowed hard, trying to get his emotions under control. He'd managed to clear the lump from his throat when Chuck walked back through the garage and handed Barry a check.

"I was going to meet up with you in a couple of days to give you this. Your mother and I want to help you and Tess out. It was just made out yesterday after I..."

Suddenly, the lump in Barry's throat was back again. He stared at the ten thousand dollar check, then looked closely at his dad's red-rimmed eyes. Suddenly, he realized what was missing. "Dad—where's your Caddy?"

Chuck waved his hand like he was shooing away a fly. He walked over and grabbed the broom, then went back to sweeping the garage. "I sold it. Like I said, your mom and I want to help you out."

Barry stalked toward his father, anxiety tying his stomach in knots.

"You sold your Caddy for us? God, Dad. That car meant everything to you. You can't do this." Barry waved the check in his father's face. "I won't take the check. Call the guy who bought it and tell him you changed your mind."

Chuck stopped sweeping and looked up at Barry. "Look, Son. When push comes to shove, it's all about family, nothing more," he said with a soft smile. "The Caddy is nothing but a bucket of bolts. Besides, Kevin Jones kept bugging the crap out of me to sell it to him so he could enter it into Hot August Nights. My family—my son and my grandkids—come first."

"But Dad..."

Chuck held up his hand and Barry stopped. He hated the fact that his father had sold something so precious, but he was also proud. This was how his father had taught him some of life's most important lessons—by setting an example. Chuck Joseph loved his family and if he could do something to help make things better, he would do it.

"This is what dad's do," Chuck said. He gently pushed Barry's hand—the hand holding the check—back against Barry's chest. "So stop arguing with me."

Teary-eyed and humbled, Barry wrapped his arms around his father and gave him a big hug.

CHAPTER 34

Tess's mood matched the gloomy day that had dawned in the Truckee Meadows. It was one of those days when Nature didn't know what it wanted to do. The sky looked like it wanted to rain but nothing developed. The sun had been hidden by the clouds all day.

Four months had passed since Triple A had pulled Barry's pickup home. Barry and Michael had worked together almost every weekend to repair the body of the vehicle. The truck was still in rough shape, but they'd managed to make it drivable. It was missing a front fender and had some dents in the front bumper, but the engine worked and the tires turned without grinding against any vital parts.

Tess watched the truck limp down the road as the men took it for a test drive. She genuinely loved and admired her husband. The man worked his butt off for his family and he was always quick to show his love for Tess. He had started a small business and had done pretty well with it until the economy slowed his progress. Tess said a brief prayer of gratitude that Barry had not been injured in the accident. She just wished that their situation was different, that somehow she could help out more. It was bad enough that her hours had been cut, but to miss out on the opportunity at Great Basin Gaming because of their *credit*? She was so frustrated she couldn't think straight. She was more than capable of performing the job, but had been denied the chance because Nation One couldn't get their act together. She just felt so helpless.

She headed back into the house. One thing she could do was to check in with Thorn and Associates to see if there was any progress on their appeal. She pulled out her cell phone and dialed the number.

"The number you are trying to reach is disconnected or no longer in service. If you think you dialed..."

Thinking she had punched in the number incorrectly, Tess double checked the number and tried it again. She got the same message. She felt like someone had just punched her in the stomach. She went into the living room and dug out Gary Thorn's business card. She dialed the man's cell and impatiently waited. Gary picked up on the first ring. *Thank God.*

"Gary, am I glad you picked up. I got this message that your number had been disconnected…"

"Who is this?" Thorn asked.

"It's me. Tess Joseph."

"Oh… Sorry, Tess. Didn't you get the e-mail we sent out last week? We're out of business."

Tess's mouth went dry. "Out of business? Why? What happened?"

"Well…you see…I had a silent partner who refused to fund the business anymore, so I had no choice but to close the doors."

"But, what about our modification?" Tess exclaimed, her voice cracking. "We were in the middle of an appeal!"

"I'll tell you, Tess." Thorn sounded like he was explaining something to a child. "Nation One is one tough bastard. They're almost impossible to work with. That's why so many people are walking away from their homes, even homeowners who have a valid case and meet all of the requirements for a loan modification. Nation One beats them down until the homeowners can't fight anymore. Have you and Barry discussed the fact that it might be easier to walk away?"

Tess rolled her eyes. This was not what she wanted to hear. "Yes, we've discussed it," she said through clenched teeth. "But we wanted to at least *try* for a modification. It seems a little early in the game to just give up. Where do you suggest we go from here?"

"Sorry, Tess. I don't have any other ideas. You and Barry will have to deal with Nation One on your own. Good luck to you."

Chapter 35

*D*EAL WITH *Nation One on your own*. Right. Just thinking about Thorn's off-handed comment made Tess's blood boil and now was not a good time to be distracted. It was another blustery fall day in Reno. Driving was treacherous due to all the dead sagebrush blowing across the road. Cars unlucky enough to hit a piece would often drag the dead sage all the way home. She was fighting the wind and watching for sagebrush on her way home from Go Tech. Just as she turned onto South Meadows Parkway, the Billy Joel song, "We Didn't Start the Fire," ended and a commercial break came on:

"Are you having problems making your house payment? Making Homes Affordable can help. Making Homes Affordable is the government initiative that helps struggling homeowners get mortgage relief through a variety of programs that aid in mortgage modifications, interest rate reductions, refinancing, deferred payments, or transitioning out of your home while avoiding fore-closure. Just call one simple number—800-773-9999—or your mortgage provider to find out if you are eligible for the Making Homes Affordable Program. Quit your worrying and take action now before you lose your home completely."

Hope washed over Tess. Was this what they'd been looking for? Could they meet the program requirements needed to stay in their home? *What do we have to lose,* she thought. *We might as well work with the government instead of a do-nothing bank.* After all, Nation One wasn't doing them any favors.

As soon as she got home, she grabbed her laptop and went to the dining room table. She hopped on the Internet to check out the Making Homes Affordable program. She was excited to see that a qualified home-owner's payment could not be any bigger than one-third of the owner's gross income.

She grabbed her cell phone and called Barry. She told him about the radio ad and how she was online, checking the requirements.

"Go for it, honey. Give them a call. What do we have to lose?" Barry said.

"Exactly what I was thinking." Tess could see him smiling in her mind. "Consider it done."

She called the toll free number and was connected to someone named Lisa. Lisa was very nice and understanding. "It seems like you should be able to get some assistance, Mrs. Joseph, so all you have to do is call your mortgage provider and tell them you called us and that you want to apply."

"You mean I have to call those do-nothing people at Nation One? I don't believe it!" Tess put a hand on top of her head. Not only did they have to jump through more hoops to get their financial situation taken care of, they still had to deal with Nation One. "Why didn't they tell me about this program to begin with?" Tess asked.

"I couldn't tell you, Mrs. Joseph," Lisa said.

Tess thanked Lisa, and after saying goodbye, called Nation One. She immediately was put on hold, and sat there listening to messages over and over again about how they prided themselves on customer service and how they cared about each and every one of their customers.

"That is the biggest bunch ob bullshit I've ever heard," Tess said when she'd heard the recording for the fifth time. She stomped over to the refrigerator and pulled out the last beer.

"Crap!" She'd need a hell of a lot more to settle herself down after dealing with these assholes. She finally got through to some guy named Rick. She tried to remain calm. Getting upset would get her nowhere with these desk jockeys.

"Yes, Rick, I would like to inquire about the Making Homes Affordable Program. Can you help me with that?"

"Yes, we can. One moment please," Rick said.

The line went dead.

Tess was furious. She took several deep breaths to calm her nerves, took another swig of beer, and called again. Luckily, this time her call was answered after only having to listen to their recorded message three times. She was immediately transferred.

After being transferred, a lady named Penny picked up. Tess introduced herself and didn't waste any time with pleasantries. "I would like to inquire about the Making Homes Affordable Program. Can you help me?"

"Have you considered our short sale program, Mrs. Joseph?"

"No, I really would like to stay in our home."

"Are you sure? It is a great program."

"I'm sure. I would like apply for the Making Homes Affordable Program." Tess could hear a big frustrated breath from the other end of the phone.

"Why can't you make the payments, Mrs. Joseph?" Penny asked in a stern voice.

Tess could feel the woman's tension through the phone. She tried to remain calm. Who knew what was setting this woman off? Maybe she'd had a rough day listening to homeowners like Tess complain.

She explained about her reduction of hours and Barry's hardware business being down as well as the poor overall economy in the Reno area.

The woman finally relented. "Okay, I'll send you out a packet of paperwork. You have to fill it out completely and get it back to us by the twenty-third of this month."

"Thank you, Penny, I appreciate it," Tess said, feeling like she'd just won a major battle. She shouldn't have to pull teeth just so they'd send her a damn packet, but she'd done it. Tess smiled and raised the half-finished beer in a silent toast.

CHAPTER 36

AFTER RECEIVING the Making Homes Affordable packet, filling out the paperwork, and sending it in, nothing happened. Tess and Barry re-applied three months later and still heard nothing from Nation One. Tess made repeated follow-up calls and Nation One never responded.

Ten months later Barry and Tess were still going around in circles with different customer service representatives from Nation One. At last count they were on the sixth representative who was supposedly "in charge of the account." They had hoped that a governmental agency of some sort would step in and help them. Every letter they sent to Nation One was copied to the secretary of state of Nevada, the governor of Nevada, a United States senator, the United States secretary of commerce, the secretary of housing and urban development, and of course, the president of the United States.

So many actions had taken place, but nothing was working. Most of the calls and correspondence had been handled by Tess since she was only working part-time. Too bad she wasn't getting paid for dealing with Nation One—that was becoming its own full-time job!

It was a typical December day in Reno, partly cloudy with a light breeze. In northern Nevada, no one really knew what kind of weather was coming. Four inches of snow had fallen overnight, but the daytime temperature was warmer than normal, around forty-five degrees, and the roads were slushy with the remnants of last night's winter storm. The drive home from the hardware store was treacherous with most cars creeping along trying to avoid the cars that were sliding. The trouble with Reno having a mixture of people from different towns and cities was that some didn't know how to drive in winter conditions.

Barry kept his speed down and his eyes on the rest of the traffic. His stomach burned, but it wasn't from the driving. He'd just found out that his neighbor, Barney Nelson, had been foreclosed on. When he added the constant foreclosures he heard about to Michael's horror stories about the real estate market, he couldn't keep the fear of losing his house from overwhelming him.

"God, we want to make the payments. We are good people. We just want to get this whole thing settled and move on with our lives," Barry prayed as he drove up his driveway in his busted-up pickup. He gave the truck a pat as he slammed the door and headed into the house.

He could hear Tess out in the kitchen. He tossed his keys in the key basket. Might as well go get the news of the day. Tess was at the counter, pouring herself a glass of Bogle chardonnay.

She was in tears.

"What's going on, Tess?" He started to go to her, to put his arms around her, but her next words froze him in place.

"It's those damn people at Nation One. They lost our Dodd Frank form."

Suddenly, all the anxiety, all the fear, came rushing at him like an out-of-control avalanche. "Goddamn it, Tess. Did you forget to send the form in? Shit! A stupid move like that could cost us our home! How could you do such a stupid thing?" Barry paced back and forth, running his hands through his hair. "Now what are we supposed to do?"

"I sent it in, Barry. I swear to God I sent it in!" Tess said with a sob. "You think I want to lose the house?"

Blood pounded in Barry's ears. He wasn't listening to Tess, not really. All he could hear was Michael's voice telling him about the Nelson foreclosure. "What were you doing when you sent it in?" He pointed at the stack of paperwork they'd accumulated since starting the modification process. "I bet the paper is right there in that stack."

"No, it isn't." Tess glared at him. "I've already looked through the stack three times."

"Well, look again, damn it. It has to be here somewhere." Barry went over to the stack, yanked off the top sheet, and slammed it down on the counter. Then he did the same to the next and the next.

After he'd gone through the stack two times, Barry conceded. They decided to call off the search and ask their new contact from Nation One what to do next.

The next day, after twenty-five attempts to get in touch with their Nation One contact, someone finally called back and told them to resend everything within two days in order to qualify for the Making Homes Affordable government program.

They immediately filled out a new Dodd Frank form and overnighted it along with the accompanying paperwork to Nation One.

Chapter 37

I**T HAD BEEN** fifteen months since they'd first applied for the Making Homes Affordable program through Nation One. The Josephs were beyond frustrated with the bank. Now they were on their ninth account representative, but hope filled their hearts this time. Their current representative said she was responding directly from the Office of the President of Nation One.

Maybe writing to all those influential politicians *had* made a difference. At least that's what Tess thought—until she discovered the blogs, like NationOnesucks. com

One post talked about papers constantly being lost.

Another post was from a former Nation One employee who'd been told to lose papers like the Dodd Frank forms.

Yet another post talked about Nation One and working with this employee or that employee and how that employee had suddenly turned unhelpful or had totally disappeared.

The post that really caught their attention actually talked about the representative they were currently working with. "Oh, she works for the office of the president of Nation One," the post stated. "That doesn't mean squat. She still lost my paperwork. She never called back. What a joke."

People talked about being given the "transfer runaround" on the phone, being passed from one supervisor to another, and walking away from the homes they had lived in for over twenty years because they got tired of all the runaround.

One of the blogs stated the following:

> I just wanted to be honest and share my story. After two years spent fighting with Nation One to get a modification, I actually received the approval documents signed and notarized. Once I'd signed the papers and Nation One was processing them, they notified me that there was an issue with the documents and told me that I had to re-sign. They never sent me the new documents.

Instead they sent me a denial letter stating that the investor had changed their mind. At this point the stress had taken over my life and my wife left me. I decided to file Chapter 7 and walk away from my house. My court date is in a couple of months. I'll live in this house rent free until I am forced out and then will move on with my life. I am very comfortable with my decision now. I wish everyone who has to suffer through this process much luck!

Tess continued to read from the laptop propped open on the dining room table while Barry read over her shoulder.

They lost my paper work again. Nation One blows.

Well, they did it again. Can't get a modification because they lost the freaking paperwork. Talking to my fifth person. This time it's some loser named Tom. What happened to Frank?

I think Nation One is feeding me a line of crap by saying that I'm dealing with someone from the "Office of the President." The last three people said they were from the "Office of the President." They're all full of it.

Tess looked up at Barry. "This isn't good. What's going on? What do we do?"

Barry looked at the worry in her beautiful eyes. "I don't know, Tess. I just don't know."

CHAPTER 38

HIGH DESERT WINTERS tended less towards snow and more towards cold and dry. The dryness could cause a person to wake up in the middle of the night with a horrible thirst or a bloody nose. Many homes used humidifiers to combat the dryness.

This was the case in the Joseph house. The humming of the humidifier at night provided a white noise that usually helped lull the Josephs to sleep.

In spite of the white noise, after reading the blogs and realizing how many other people were having the same problems they were having, Tess and Barry couldn't sleep. They both lay on their backs, staring at the darkened ceiling, hoping an answer to their problems would appear. They held hands and prayed, saying their normal prayers first—asking for God's grace, letting Him know how thankful they were, asking Him to protect their family as they slept. Then Barry added another plea: "Lord, we don't understand the logic of the bank that holds our mortgage. They don't seem to want to work with us. Lord help guide them, and lend us your support through these hard financial times. We are struggling and are at the end of our rope. We ask this in your son's powerful and mighty name. Amen"

Barry rolled onto his side and looked at Tess. "Look, honey, I know you have worked your butt off dealing with the bank while I'm at the hardware store. I really appreciate what you've tried to do for us."

"It's hard to pray for the bank we despise," Tess said, rolling on her side and touching Barry's cheek with a finger.

He sighed and rolled back onto his back, sliding his right hand behind his head. "I know, but that's what good Christians are supposed to do."

Tess laid her head on his chest and put a hand on his shoulder. "Do we start to look for a place to rent, then? How long do we go on fighting them, Barry?"

"I don't know, honey. Right now we're not making the house payment so we're basically living here free." He sat up, dropping his legs over the edge of the bed. He stared at the wall, wondering what more they could do. He ran his fingers through his hair, over and over, as if he could pull an answer directly out of his skull.

Tess moved over and sat up. She put both arms around Barry's neck and rested her head on his shoulder. She kissed him on the neck. "We'll get through this. We're Josephs and Josephs are fighters. We're not letting those bastards get the best of us. Remember—this house is just bricks and mortar. We are the ones who make it a home. We can leave here and will still have a home no matter where we end up living. We're together no matter what happens."

Barry kissed her soundly and they both rolled back into bed.

CHAPTER 39

WILLIAM DARK had delivered mail for nearly sixteen years in Reno and thought he had seen almost everything. But the number of packages and letters from banks and mortgage companies he'd been delivering lately really bothered him. Dark hated to deliver bad news.

He pulled up in front of the Joseph's home and noticed he had another one of "those" packages from Nation One Bank.

"Damn it!" he said as he grabbed the certified envelope. Dark liked the Josephs. They went to his church and Tess always made cookies for him at Christmas time. Barry always took the time to stop whatever he was doing and say hello. Barry was also helping him with building plans for the new addition to his house, placing special orders for the project at the hardware store.

"Why do bad things happen to good people?" Dark grumbled as he walked up the steps and rang the doorbell. "I'm so tired of this shit."

A dog barked somewhere inside. He could see Tess through the side window. He reached into his satchel and grabbed a doggy bone as the door opened and the yellow lab stuck its head out. Dark held out the doggy treat and the lab took it gently between her teeth.

"Hi, Bill. What's up?" Tess asked.

"I have this package I need you to sign for," he said, handing the envelope to Tess.

"Okay." She looked at the envelope and didn't say anything more.

TESS SIGNED FOR the envelope, said her goodbyes, and closed the door. She stared at the envelope in her hand, unable to even think for a moment. Sierra nudged her hand and finally Tess moved. She went through the living room into the kitchen, shoving Sierra aside. She'd get the dog a treat later. Now she had to find out what was so important the bank had sent a certified letter. She grabbed a paring knife from the knife drawer. She slipped the knife in the edge of the flap, slid the knife through the envelope, and pulled out the letter inside.

Dear Mr. and Mrs. Barry Joseph,

You have fallen behind on your mortgage payments. You must bring the mortgage current. We have started the foreclosure process.

The letter blurred. Tess didn't remember reading the rest, but suddenly found herself staring at the last sentence...

We urge you to contact Nation One at 1-800-555-5555 and talk to a representative who will work with you to try to solve your current difficulty.

Contact Nation One. She started to giggle, a silly little sound she couldn't seem to stop. Then the word "foreclosure" jumped out at her and the room started to spin. Tess grabbed the back of a chair to steady herself. She tried taking deep breaths, but the room kept spinning. She edged her way around the chair and sat, trying to gather her thoughts.

CHAPTER 40

"**H**ONEY, **THEY'VE ONLY** started the foreclosure process. It's not like they'll follow through with it," Barry said, bringing Tess another glass of water. She'd been on the verge of fainting when he'd gotten home two hours ago and he wasn't sure she still wouldn't faint on him.

"But it could happen. My god, Barry. What are we going to do?" Tess took the glass, but didn't drink it.

Barry grabbed her by the shoulders and looked at her.

"We just keep doing what we have been doing."

She turned away, walked to the counter, and placed her glass down. She turned back to him, her eyes glimmering with tears. "What the hell is going on here? We can't do shit!"

"What are you talking about?" Barry asked, holding up his hands.

Tess walked closer, waving her open right hand at the room. "Open your eyes, damn it! Everything is pretty much up to date but the house. It's the only damn thing that's holding us hostage. You need a new truck—we can't buy one because our credit is shit. I don't know whether to plant a garden this year or not because we're not sure whether we will be foreclosed on. We can't replace the freakin' roof because we not only don't have the money, we don't want to throw money into a house we could be kicked out of. Same with the landscaping and painting we need to do. We should dump the carpet upstairs because the dog did her business all over it, and the patio is on its last leg. Barry, we're living in freakin' limbo!"

She looked down at the floor, looking depressed and defeated.

Barry walked up to her. He took his hand and lifted her face toward his. Then he put his hands on her shoulders and looked her in the eyes. "What do you want to do, Tess? Do you want to just leave? We live here for free, for God's sake. We might as well stay here until we are kicked out and save whatever money we can. That way we at least have a chance to make a down payment for an apartment."

"As long as they don't check our credit," Tess answered as tears poured down her cheeks.

Barry wrapped his arms around her and pulled her close. She was right—they had to do something. He just didn't know what.

CHAPTER 41

T WAS 6:07 in the morning in early March. It was twenty-five degrees outside with a light dusting of snow coating the yard. Tess crawled out of bed and threw on her sweatshirt, jeans, and tennis shoes. She briskly rubbed her upper arms, trying to generate some heat. The house was fifty-five degrees. They kept the temperature down to save on the heating bills. Tess went downstairs and let Sierra out. Then she filled the teapot, set it on the stove, and turned on the burner. While she waited for the water to heat, she went out front and picked up the morning paper. The front page headlines made her stomach hurt. The economy was continuing to tumble downward. Sixty-five percent of the homes for sale in Washoe County were distressed properties. There were families facing more horrific hardships than they were.

Tess looked up at the naked oak tree in the front yard. The tree was beautiful when in bloom and provided a lot of shade for the house. She could picture Barry raking leaves in the fall as the kids laughed and ran and jumped into the pile.

She shook her head and stalked back into the house. No use letting her mind wander. More than likely they weren't going to be around to rake leaves next fall. She walked past the gray stone fireplace and remembered the last time she'd hung stockings for Christmas. She'd turned to see Barry and Daniel frosting Christmas cookies in the kitchen as Maggie stared at the Christmas tree lights with a smile, looking back at Tess with holiday excitement sparkling in her eyes.

The memories were everywhere. She ran a finger along the dining room table, picturing the room decorated for Thanksgiving, Barry carving the turkey while Maggie and Daniel stood waiting with Chuck and Betty for a succulent piece of meat. Everyone was laughing and having a great time...

The whistling teapot snapped Tess back to reality. She ran into the kitchen and turned off the stove before lifting the tea pot and pouring boiling water over the tea bag waiting in her favorite mug. She turned around and looked at her beautiful home. The place wasn't decorated with a lot of material riches, but with love—homemade gifts from the kids and knick knacks from friends and family. She set the steaming cup on the counter and began to sob.

CHAPTER 42

BARRY AND TESS had just settled down to watch TV for the evening while the kids were out in the backyard playing. Barry sat in his recliner sipping a beer while Tess stretched out on the couch reading a Nicholas Sparks novel. The KOLO 6:30 news played in the background. Suddenly the news anchor said, "This just in: the attorney general of Nevada, along with the governor's office, has just introduced Nevada's Hardest Hit Fund, a special fund for homeowners who have been hit hard during the down economy. The state of Nevada is one of five states selected to receive special treasury funds specifically slated to help homeowners who are financially upside down in their home mortgages. A special nonprofit corporation has been approved to oversee the fund, under the direction of the Nevada Housing Division. This new fund provides four programs to assist those Nevada homeowners who are at high risk of default or foreclosure."

"We have to check this out." Barry sat up so fast he bumped the stand next to his chair and knocked his beer bottle over.

"I'll call tomorrow morning and see what we have to do," Tess said, grabbing the towel she'd just folded from the laundry basket next to the couch and tossing it to Barry.

THE FOLLOWING MORNING Tess called the Nevada Housing Division and got the number for the Nevada Affordable Housing Assistance Corporation. She kept getting a busy signal, but was determined to get through. On her ninth try, she finally got through to someone.

"NAHAC. My name is Sharon. How can I help you?" said the sweet-sounding voice on the other end of the line.

Tess took a deep breath. "Hi, my name is Tess Joseph, and my husband and I are trying to get a modification. We heard about your program. How do we qualify for the funds that are available to help us out?"

"Your lender should know all about this and they should be able to help you with this new program. Who is your lender?" Sharon asked.

"Nation One," Tess said.

"Just call them. They should know all about it. Nevada is one of five states that qualified for this program."

"OK, thanks," Tess said. She gritted her teeth as she hung up. Not only did she have to make another phone call, she had to call the very same folks who'd been causing them problems all along. She looked at the carefully documented list of people she had talked with so far.

"I wonder who our representative is this week?" she muttered to herself, looking through the pages of notes. After a minute she found the name Darren Kiper. Darren was the sixteenth representative they'd had in the past twenty months. Who knew where the others had disappeared to?

Tess called and left a message. After almost three hours someone finally called back. "Hi, my name is Nate Bloomberg. I'm your newly assigned representative for Nation One. How can I help you?"

"What happened to Darren Kiper? I thought he was our representative."

"I'm sorry, Mrs. Joseph. I don't know the answer to that question. I am your representative and I will be more than happy to help you."

"Okay, Nate. I would like to talk to you about Nevada's Hardest Hit fund," Tess said.

"Nevada's what?"

"Nevada's Hardest Hit fund. It was all over the news yesterday. I called the main office and was told that my lender would know about this."

"I'm sorry, Mrs. Joseph, but I've never heard of such a fund."

"Look, it was all over the news. I just got off the phone with them a few hours ago and was told that you would know how we go about qualifying."

"Hold on. Let me check with my supervisor."

Tess made a cup of tea while she patiently waited. Someone *had* to know what she needed to do. After about five minutes, Bloomberg finally came back on the line.

"I'm sorry, Mrs. Joseph. No one here has ever heard of such a fund."

"This is a brand-new program…," Tess started.

Bloomberg interrupted. "I assure you, Mrs. Joseph. Nation One is always up on the latest programs. I am well trained and I would know about this program if such a program existed. I'm confused, Mrs. Joseph. It says here that you do not want a modification and would be interested in our short sale program."

"Who put that crap in there? Wait. I am Mrs. Barry Joseph of Reno, Nevada. Do you have the right person?"

Bloomberg went over the social security and account numbers to verify that he was talking to the right person.

"That is me, Nate, but I never said I didn't want a modification. In fact, we've been trying for almost two years to get a modification."

"Well, that is what it says here."

"Please make a note in your computer that we want a modification. We have no intention of short selling."

"I will, Mrs. Joseph. Is there anything else I can help you with?"

"Damn straight, there is. Get your poop in a pile and look up Nevada's Hardest Hit fund." Tess slammed down the phone and pounded the kitchen counter in frustration. They just couldn't seem to win.

CHAPTER 43

THE DAY WAS LIKE any typical late spring day in Northern Nevada. The trees had bloomed and the cherry blossoms had reached their peak and were starting to wither. Residents with pools were getting them ready for the upcoming hot summer days. May was the perfect time of year for northern Nevada.

Out in the front yard Barry was pacing back and forth across the front lawn, pushing the gas mower in front of him. The tiny front yard took less than a half hour to mow and trim and he was almost halfway done. As he turned to make another pass, a man pulled up across the street in a two-year-old white Chevy Tahoe and sat staring at Barry as he mowed.

About the time Barry was ready to go find out what the man wanted, the guy climbed out of his truck and headed his way. The man looked to be around fifty with graying brown hair. Barry quickly noted the medium build and decided he could take the guy if he had to. The way the guy had been just sitting in his truck made Barry's skin itch. He turned off the mower as the guy stopped on the opposite side of the fence. "Can I help you?"

The lips of the man could barely be seen through the poorly trimmed Fu Manchu mustache. "I'm Warren Brady of Brady Investigation. We were hired by Nation One. Are you Barry Joseph?"

"Yes, what's going on here?" The itchy feeling moved from Barry's skin to his stomach.

"No big deal, Mr. Joseph. The bank just wanted to make sure the house was still occupied."

"Why the hell wouldn't it be occupied? My family has lived here for over ten years and we intend to be here for many more, so you can just tell that bank to get their act together or they're going to be sorry they ever messed with the Joseph family!"

"Just doing my job, Mr. Joseph. Excuse me but I have to go take a look at a couple more houses." The man turned around and headed back to his truck. Barry looked up to find old Bob Dugan looking over at him.

"Everything okay, Barry?" yelled Dugan.

"Ah...yeah, Bob. Everything is fine."

Barry started up the lawn mower and finished his job in the yard without another look in Bob Dugan's direction.

P<small>ART</small> 3

FACING
THE
BULLY

Chapter 44

CHUCK JOSEPH was up at dawn. He stared out the kitchen window, cup of coffee warming his hands, and frowned at the snow covering the trees of his backyard. Looked like they'd gotten two to four inches of wet snow last night. Spring could be so unpredictable in the high desert. Snow this late in the spring was rare, but not unheard of. At least he'd remembered to fill the old bird feeders before he'd gone to bed. It looked like the quail were very happy.

He looked down as Betty took hold of his arm and smiled. "What are your plans for the day?" she asked.

The snow would eventually melt as all spring snows tended to do, but he didn't want a slushy mess in his driveway. It would probably turn cold overnight, turning the slop into an icy nightmare. "Guess I'd better get out there and get the old snowblower started."

"But what about breakfast, honey?" Betty asked.

"Not yet. Wait until I get done with the driveway," Chuck said, walking over to the coffee maker. He poured another cup of coffee, kissed his wife on the forehead, and headed out the door.

Outside the air was still crisp. He set his cup aside and lit up a cigarette before pulling out his trusty old snowblower. He tried to start the blower but it wouldn't turn over. He used a couple of tricks he'd learned over the years, even tried dipping the tip of the spark plug in gasoline, but the blower refused to start.

Maybe the spark plug didn't need to be dipped, maybe it needed to be replaced. He could run down to the hardware store and get a new plug from Barry. Chuck groaned and lit another cigarette. He frowned down into depths of his cold coffee. Before he could get to Barry's store, he had to clear a path for his 2001 Ford F150. He could probably get the truck out without shoveling, but that would pack down the snow and make it even harder to clear when he got back home. So he pulled out an old snow shovel and began to push and throw snow out of the way.

What had started out wet was even wetter and heavier due to the rising temperatures. By nightfall, the mess would be even harder to move. It would harden and turn to ice overnight and he did not want Betty walking on an icy mess.

He was halfway down his thirty-foot driveway when pain stabbed his chest. He dropped the shovel, his left arm gone suddenly numb. He fell to his knees and glanced one last time at the majestic snow-covered Sierra Nevada mountain range. A blue jay squawked overhead as Chuck Barry's heart finally gave out.

Chapter 45

His father's death hit Barry hard. He couldn't sleep. He couldn't eat. He could barely drag himself out of bed. Tess had finally insisted he see a doctor, so here he was, sitting in an exam room, staring out the window and wondering just how the sun could shine so bright when the world was coming to an end.

Dr. Jorgenson had always been a kind doctor, a quality that made him unique compared to the other doctors Barry had seen through the years. Jorgenson really cared about his patients and had taken care of the Joseph family for as long as Barry could remember. He'd known Chuck for a long time, had known Chuck was dying…

"Have you eaten today, Barry?" Dr. Jorgenson's voice was loud, insistent, like Tess's voice when she'd asked him a question several times. Barry blinked and looked at the doctor, trying to focus.

"I don't think so," Barry said. He thought a moment, struggling to remember just when he'd last eaten. "No."

"Are you sleeping at all?"

"No," Barry replied with a shudder. Every time he closed his eyes he saw his father lying cold and still in that padded coffin.

"I'm sorry about your father," Jorgenson said softly. Barry stared at his hands, unable to look the doctor in the eye.

"Look at me, Barry," Dr. Jorgenson said.

Barry glanced up, then dropped his gaze again. "It isn't only Dad," he finally said. His voice cracked. "It's my business, the house, trying to figure out how to make ends meet…" Barry wiped his eyes, then stared at his wet fingers.

"I know how hard it is…"

Barry glared at the doctor. "You don't know anything," he snapped. "Have you ever wanted to die, Doctor? Well, I want to die. Everyone is expecting something from me: the bank, my family, my customers. And in the middle of this…this…mess, Dad has to up and die. What's Mom going to do now? I can't help her. Hell, I can't even help myself. Dad looked so peaceful there in that coffin, like he didn't have a care in the world. Maybe it's time I joined him."

"I can tell you one thing, my boy." Dr. Jorgenson went over to the small counter and pulled out a prescription pad.

"What's that?" Barry asked, more out of politeness than curiosity.

"Death is not an option." Dr. Jorgenson scribbled something on the pad and walked back over to Barry. "Your family desperately needs you right now. I've known you ever since you were a baby and you've never been one to give up. You're not giving up now. I'm going to start you on this medication today and then you're going to see a friend of mine, Dr. Allison Daily. She's the best in the business. I'll give her a call today and see how soon we can get you in."

He gave Barry's back a friendly pat. "Meanwhile, you're going fill this prescription, then go home, have something to eat, and lie down for a bit. I know it's difficult, especially without your father. Chuck was a good friend and a man who loved the Lord. My thoughts are with your mother as well. Please pass along my deepest sympathies to her."

"I will, Dr. Jorgenson. Thank you," Barry said. He'd felt like he was teetering on the brink of an endless black hole when he'd confessed his desire to die. Now he didn't feel anything. It was like he was at the movies watching someone else talk to the doctor and say all the appropriate words. But words didn't matter anymore. Nothing mattered anymore. He stared at the prescription in his hand. Nothing.

Chapter 46

I T WAS A WEEK after his father's funeral and Barry was still feeling depressed. He had been having such a hard time functioning at work that he decided to stay home for a bit and try to get himself together emotionally.

Barry wasn't just wallowing in pity for himself. He was worried about his mother. He and Tess had been taking turns staying overnight at Betty's house to help her get used to Chuck not being around. Everything in the house seemed to hold some kind of memory for his mother. It crushed Barry to see his mother cry. He discussed it with Tess and together they decided to remove Chuck's things. If his mother objected, she didn't say anything.

It was Sunday afternoon, and while the kids played in Betty's backyard, Barry and Tess went through

Chuck's belongings. Tess took charge since both Barry and Betty were not much into doing this task.

As Tess was sorting through Chuck's dresser drawers, Barry was pulling clothes from the closet and placing them into garbage bags. Many clothes and unused things were going to the Reno Sparks Gospel Mission Thrift stores but there were items that had personal value. These things were set aside. After Barry finished with the bedroom closet, he moved to the hall closet just around the corner. He slowly pulled out box after box and went through them. Betty stood beside him, fondly commenting about this item and that. She pointed over his shoulder at a wooden box on the middle shelf.

"Barry, honey!" she said.

Barry looked up. "What is it, Mom?"

She reached for the box. "Barry, this box is to go to you. It has some medals your father was awarded in the Navy as well as a few other items. Look at this." She pulled the box partway out, reached into it, and pulled out an old pocket watch with a gold chain attached. "It was your great-grandfather Malcolm Joseph's watch. It has been in the family for years and it keeps getting passed down. It's yours now, Barry."

Barry took the watch from his mother. It wasn't running. He remembered his father using the watch on very special occasions and started to tear up.

"You may want to take it to a watchmaker and get it cleaned. It was still running the last time your father had it out," Betty said with a grin. She looked back into the box and gasped, then pulled out an unframed photo and started to cry.

Barry put his arm around his mother. Tess did the same. Betty held out the picture for them to see. It was a twenty-some-year-old Chuck in a Navy uniform standing in front of a huge ship.

"It's going to be okay, Betty. We're here for you," Tess said, putting her head against Betty's. Betty handed the photo to Barry. He slid the photo into his shirt pocket without saying a word and turned back to the closet.

AFTER THEY'D FINISHED sorting the majority of Chuck's items, they loaded the clothes that were going to the mission thrift stores into the back of Barry's truck. He put his father's wooden box in the passenger seat.

Tess called Daniel and Maggie in from the backyard. The children ran in and gave their grandmother a hug. As Daniel pulled back Betty looked at him with a smile. "Now, Barry, who's your little friend?"

Tess looked at the children. Maggie and Daniel looked back, their foreheads wrinkled in worry.

"Mommy, why doesn't Grandma know who we are?" Maggie asked, looking up at Tess.

Tess put her arm around Betty. "Grandma is a little confused right now."

"Of course, I know who you are," Betty said, seeming to gather herself. "Come on, kids. Let's see if Grandma has any cookies for you."

Betty and the kids went into the kitchen.

Barry and Tess looked at each other. Tess looked up at Barry and whispered. "Not good."

Barry closed his eyes. He couldn't take it anymore. He just couldn't.

CHAPTER 47

TUESDAY STARTED OFF the same as any other week-
day. Barry looked in on Daniel and Maggie and
gave them both kisses goodbye, then grabbed his metal
coffee mug and gave Tess a big hug and a kiss. He went
out and climbed into his pickup truck and turned the
key. No reason to be in a rush—he'd had Brad, his assistant manager, open the store so he could take his time.

He looked over at the wooden box sitting in the
passenger seat and thought about how his father had
always been there for him. He thought about the good
times, especially his baseball-playing days, and how
in bad times Chuck had always come through. He
remembered the look on his father's face when he'd
handed Barry the check from the sale of his Caddy.
Tears flooded Barry's vision, coming so fast and hard,

he pulled over to the side of the road and sat there until the tears slowed and he could see. He pulled out the family pocket watch, stared at it a moment, then put the watch in his pants pocket. Then he took a deep breath and pulled back into traffic.

Five minutes later, Barry pulled into the Nation One parking lot. He reached into his breast pocket and pulled out the picture of his father in the Navy. He looked at the photo for a long moment, then put it back in his pocket and climbed out of the truck.

The Joseph family never gave up. No matter the situation, they gave everything they had to give.

Barry pulled open the giant glass door and went into the bank. He was greeted by a bright-eyed, blond-haired teller wearing a name tag that said *Mindy.* "How can I help you?" Mindy asked.

Barry cleared his throat. "I would like to see Sue Bennett, please."

"Do you have an appointment?"

"No," Barry glanced around, taking in all the customers standing in line, the tellers busy at their windows. "Look, it's important that I see her."

"And your name?"

"Barry Joseph."

Barry could feel his father's presence as if the man was standing next to him, lending his encouragement.

The young lady girl went into Bennett's glass office. He could see her speaking to Sue Bennett as the young girl pointed at him. The woman looked at Barry, then gave the girl a nod. Mindy smiled as Bennett stood and waved at him.

Barry walked slowly back to the office and sat down. A calmness settled over him. He felt as if he was meant to do this. As if this time, things were finally going to work out.

"Mr. Joseph," Bennett said. "I have an appointment in five minutes. Mindy said it was important. How can I help you?"

"I would like you to get on the phone with your corporate office so we can hammer out a modification."

"Look, Mr. Joseph, I told you before I would like to help you out, but this is a matter…"

Without blinking an eye, Barry pulled the .38 Special out from under his jacket. "Oh, I think you can call someone."

Bennett stared at him.

"Keep your hands where I can see them," Barry said, realizing he sounded like a movie actor. He tried again. "Look, Sue, I'm not here to hurt anyone or rob the bank. I just want to talk to someone from your corporate office. A real person. Someone who can help us get this modification through."

He glanced over and saw Mindy staring at them, wide-eyed. He'd wanted to do this quiet and simple, but he'd forgotten the offices were glass. Now he didn't have a choice. "You're going to march out there and have everyone step outside while we work this out. Tell them not to touch the alarm, and everyone will be okay. I want to make payments, I want to work this thing out. I just need someone from your corporate office to help me."

Bennett inched out from behind her desk and stepped in front of him. All the color had drained from her face and he could see her hands shaking. Together they walked into the bank's lobby.

"Can everyone come out from behind the counter, please?" Bennett said in a shaky voice.

The customers in line looked at Bennett, many of them frowning. Barry kept the gun's muzzle pressed against Bennett's lower back, out of the customers' sight.

Bennett tried again "I'm sorry, folks. We have to close early. You'll have to leave."

The tellers came out from behind the counter, looking curiously at Bennett. One by one the other bank officers emerged from their offices.

"Sue, what's going on?" the branch manager asked.

"He has a gun, Jim. You all have to leave."

Barry could hear the tension in her voice.

The manager just stared. "But you don't know the combination to the safe and—"

"He doesn't want money."

"What?"

"He wants a modification."

Barry took a deep breath to keep himself calm. He just wanted to get this thing over with. "You heard the lady. Get the hell out of here and no one gets hurt," he said, holding the gun out in the open. His heart threatened to explode from his chest as he pointed the barrel at Bennett's head. Why did they have to make things so hard?

Feet shuffled across the tile floor as everyone filed out of the building.

Barry eased the gun down and looked at Bennett. "Looks like you got some dialing to do."

CHAPTER 48

BENNETT WALKED BACK to her office, picked up the phone, and pushed a button. Barry wasn't surprised to see that she had corporate headquarters on her speed dial.

"Dan, this is Sue in Reno. I have a problem and I need your help. I have a man here who's holding a gun on me. He wants a modification."

He waved the gun barrel at the phone. "Put it on speaker."

She reached over and punched another button. "Yeah, right, Sue—"

"Damn it, Dan, I'm not kidding. We've cleared the building..." She glanced up at Barry, her eyes wide.

"She's not kidding," Barry said. "Just keep being a smart ass and you'll see just how serious this is."

"Oh," the guy on the other end—Dan—stammered. "Ah…sorry…what is his name…your name, sir?"

"Barry Joseph."

"Okay, Mr. Joseph. My name is Dan Evans and I'm vice president of the mortgage division of Nation One Bank. Look, we don't want anyone hurt—"

"Nor do I, Mr. Evans. I just want to talk to someone from your corporation who can help me get a modification." Barry's voice rose in frustration. "You dumb asses keep losing our documents. You make us jump through hoops, then you lie and cheat, hoping that we'll give up. As you can see—we're not giving up. I want to get this thing settled. Look, I want to make payments, I want to keep my house. Can you help me or not?"

"I'm not sure what I can do, Mr. Joseph."

Barry waved the gun at Bennett, raising his eyebrows and tilting his head toward the phone.

"Goddamn it, Dan. Get this man a modification!" Bennett yelled.

"Ok, Mr. Joseph," Evans said, his voice quavering. "You made your point. Let's get started."

Barry knew his time was limited. Any minute now his whole world was likely to collapse. He had to get as much done as he could before the police arrived. Would they shoot him, he wondered as he listened to Evans and his secretary yell at each other while they tried to pull up his records. Barry had already decided it didn't matter if he died. At least he'd drawn attention to Nation One and their plight. The press would have a field day when they got hold of his story…

"Got it," Evans said, triumph in his voice. "It looks like everything is in order."

"What about reducing our principle," Barry asked. His mouth went suddenly dry as he watched police cars pull up in front of the bank. Blue and red lights flashed across the wall.

"I'm not sure…"

"Look—you bastards received all that money from the government for just this reason. You're putting it in your own pockets or something. Why else wouldn't you want to reduce the principle?"

"You're right, Mr. Joseph. We can reduce your principal. I'd forgotten about the government program."

Like hell he had. Barry swallowed as he saw the back of a black van open, releasing a horde of helmeted men onto the street. He wiped his suddenly sweaty hand on his pant leg.

"I've put my signature on the modification documents, Mr. Joseph, and my secretary has notarized it."

"Great." Barry licked his lips. They were so close…

"All we need now is your signature, Mr. Joseph, and we'll be done. I'll have my secretary send it over via e-mail," Evans said.

The front door of the bank burst open at the same time a line of men swept in from the back. The sound of tromping boots echoed through the building. Barry stared at all the guns pointed his way as someone yelled, "Drop the gun!"

Barry held out the gun and dropped it as he fell to his knees. He'd been so close. Only a few more minutes and Tess and the children wouldn't have had to worry anymore.

Someone wrenched his hands behind his back and he felt the bite of cold steel as handcuffs were snapped into place. He stared at the bumps on the carpet. All the anticipation—all the fear—was gone. Once again, he felt nothing.

Somewhere behind him a deep voice was reading him his rights. "You have the right to remain silent. You have…"

CHAPTER 49

Barry Joseph sat in the Washoe County jail on Parr Boulevard, staring at the bars and wondering what he'd just done. Not only did he feel trapped, he felt violated. After the finger printing, shower, full body search, and a change into the typical orange prison jumpsuit, they'd escorted him to a cell and slid the door closed. Nothing sounded so final as the closing of that door. He sat on his cot with thoughts running endlessly through his mind.

Dam it, Joseph! Have you lost your mind?

Over and over the thoughts rolled through his head.

What about Tess and the kids?

Who's going to take care of the hardware store?

What about Mom? Tess can check in on her…maybe even stay with her.

The thought of Tess and what she was going through made his stomach ache.

I was just trying to save our home, he told himself. *The same home those greedy bullies were trying to take away.*

You took the bull by the horn, Joseph. Took the fight to the bullies. And they were going to give you the modification. Just a few more minutes and they would have done it.

He scrubbed his palms hard on the orange fabric covering his legs.

What the hell are you talking about? You pulled a gun on someone. You broke the law. You put everything at risk— your family, your store, your reputation.

Barry clenched his hands into tight fists, his eyes burned, and a huge lump sat in the middle of his throat. He got up and paced back and forth in the tiny nine-by-six-foot cell. He could hardly see through the tears blurring his vision. Would his family ever forgive him? Would Tess?

CHAPTER 50

TESS WAS full of mixed emotions. Part of her was scared for Barry, worried about him being in jail. Another part of her was furious, wondering how he could do such a stupid thing. How many times had they talked about how people make the home, not the building? She was also embarrassed, trying to fight her way through the media circus parked around their house.

Tess followed a female deputy sheriff through the dark halls of the Washoe County Jail. She'd been blindsided when Barry called and told her what he'd done. She'd had to wait most of the day to see him. She was scared, no question about it. The place was stale and militaristic, their footsteps echoing in the hall like they were walking through an empty building. She was shown into a room with several chairs and a partition. She gingerly sat in the chair, looking through bullet-proof glass at Barry as he came through a heavy metal door on the other side of the glass. He was dressed in an orange jumpsuit, his hands and ankles in chains. Barry sat down as the deputy that had led him in undid his hand cuffs. Barry grabbed the phone and held it to his ear.

She picked up her phone and said the first thing that came to mind. "What were you thinking?" She swallowed hard, but couldn't stop her tears. She reached into her purse for a tissue to wipe her eyes, then looked up at Barry. He looked so miserable. So defeated. She shook her head, feeling so sorry for him. She forgot her anger, wanting only to wrap her arms around him. To tell him everything was going to be okay. She blew her nose. It wasn't going to be okay. Not for a long, long time.

"I don't know." Barry shrugged. He looked away, as if seeking the answers on the wall. "I guess I'd had enough. I hated having someone else control our lives. Nation One controlled our credit. They harassed us. They offered hope and then pulled the rug out from under us. They wouldn't even talk to us. I just took matters in my own hands, I guess. I wanted that damn modification so bad." Barry looked as tired as she felt.

Tess shook her head again, her anger returning. She slammed her hand on the counter so hard her palm stung. "But what about your family, damn it? Didn't you even think about us? Did you forget about Daniel and Maggie? Did you forget about me?"

She put her face in her hands and started to cry. She was scared for Barry and worried about the kids.

Barry bit his lower lip and finally looked at her. "Dad always taught me to stand up to bullies. That's exactly what I did."

"Why you?" Tess asked.

"No one else was doing it. You saw all those blog posts. We weren't the only ones being given the runaround, but no one else had the balls to stand up to those assholes."

"So, what are we going to do now, Barry?" The tears started falling again as Tess stared at her husband. "What are we going to do?"

CHAPTER 51

BARRY JOSEPH'S arrest made headline news. News stations called in guests and editorials theorized about the incident. Most people sympathized with Barry Joseph, claiming the situation was a case of David versus Goliath, and confirming how hard it was to get the banks to talk to you when it came to getting a loan modification. The phones rang off the hook at the local talk radio stations as folks called in to discuss how terrible the situation was. Many called Barry a "nut job" while most called him a hero.

On KKOH, the conservative talk show host discussed the situation in detail, going over all the pros and cons. The responses were varied:

"Who can blame the guy? You know how hard it is to get the banks to talk to you."

"The banks are greedy bastards. They don't give a shit about you. They just want more money."

"Did you see how much of a bonus Nation One's CEO received last year? And we bailed those bastards out with our tax dollars?"

"Look, the Josephs signed a contract like everyone else. They are obligated to pay the mortgage they signed up for."

"That guy had a gun and should get the maximum time."

"I hope others don't follow suit."

"The man's father just died. He probably went off the deep end."

A rally started outside the jail as a crowd slowly gathered. The press had a field day as they interviewed different people amid the shouts of "Free Joseph!" and "Nation One is Greedy!"

Chapter 52

Judge Harold Bloom determined that there was enough evidence to hold Barry Joseph over for trial. The Truckee Meadows area was buzzing about what happened.

Mark Sheehan, the Washoe County district attorney, sent his assistant district attorney, Rochelle Chandler, to handle the trial. Sheehan had been getting a lot of heat about the upcoming trial with many residents expressing sympathy for the defendant. Sheehan tried to get the trial moved to Elko, but Bloom dismissed his request for change of venue. But Sheehan had a job to do and that was to keep Joseph in jail.

Leonard Gray, Joseph's defense attorney, went to see Chandler, hoping to get a plea bargain for his client. They met in her Sierra Avenue office. The office was in a rustic brick building built in 1922, a building the city had wanted to tear down for years. The building was saved from demolition when the residents filed petition after petition to prevent the destruction of the historical property. The city decided instead to use the building to house their district attorney offices.

"Come on, Rochelle, you know everyone will be on your case if you send this guy to prison for life. He's a hero. Someone who finally did something everyone in the nation has wanted to do." Gray smoothed the crease of his pant leg as he watched Rochelle Chandler's face.

"You know we can't have people running into banks with guns and threatening other people's lives just because they're pissed off at the bank."

"This is a very unusual circumstance. The man's father just died and he's been under financial stress for almost two years. I'm sure the DA would be willing to offer Joseph a plea bargain. The guy has a wife and two kids."

"The DA wants this man behind bars, Counselor. At this point, he is not inclined to offer any deals."

"At least drop the hostage charge. You don't have the evidence to back that one up and you know it."

Chandler looked at him for a long moment. Then she gave a quick nod. "We'll take that under consideration, but I'm not making you any promises. As for the rest, your man is going to pay for what he's done. The DA will see to that."

Gray stood. No use wasting more time and risking the one concession he might have won for his client. A couple of years in prison was better than life behind bars. If he played his cards right, though, if he kept with the plan he'd concocted sometime during the night, his client wouldn't spend anymore time behind bars. He held out his hand. "Convince the DA to drop the hostage charge and I'll buy you the best steak dinner in Reno, Rochelle."

She shook her head and frowned. Gray grinned. "See you in court."

CHAPTER 53

THE WASHOE COUNTY courtroom was full on the day of Barry's trial. The forty-degree outside temperatures were reflected throughout the gray marble floors of the building. The day felt as cold as Chandler's meeting with Gray.

The courtroom buzzed as the audience watched Barry walk in. He kept his gaze focused straight ahead, embarrassed and ashamed to be the center of all the attention. He'd just sat down at the table beside his attorney when the side door opened.

"All rise!" yelled the elderly bailiff as Judge Harold Bloom walked in. Everyone in the courtroom stood as the judge stepped up to the bench and took his seat.

"You may be seated," the judge said. He looked to be about fifty-five and had a stern, no-nonsense look on his face.

Barry was dressed in a gray suit with a black-and-white striped tie. He nervously rubbed his legs and took deep breaths to calm down as he glanced at the jury. His attorney had filled him in on the makeup of the jury. The thirteen members were a mixture of young and old: a CEO of a mining company, a secretary, two elderly housewives, two college students, a drugstore worker, a food sales representative, a retired nurse, an unemployed factory worker, a casino bartender, an insurance adjuster, and a middle manager of a chemical company who was the foreman of the jury.

Judge Bloom gave the jury their instructions and went over some ground rules with the audience, stressing that there was to be no cameras, traditional or cell phone, in the courtroom.

The charges were read out loud. Barry Joseph faced two charges: aiming a firearm at a human being, a gross misdemeanor punishable by a minimum jail sentence of one year and/or a fine of up to $2,000; and drawing a deadly weapon in a threatening manner, a misdemeanor punishable by a year in jail and a fine of not more than $1,000. The felony crime of taking a person hostage had been dropped, though Barry wasn't quite sure why. There seemed to be a confusion as to whether or not Sue Bennett was actually a hostage or not. That was one argument Barry's attorney claimed to have won out of court. Barry was scared enough facing the two current charges; he was definitely happy not to be facing life in prison.

The judge looked directly at Barry before glancing at his attorney. "How does the defendant plead?"

"The defendant pleads not guilty, Your Honor. The defense intends to prove the defendant was acting under irresistible impulse."

Spectators mumbled as the judge raised an eyebrow. "An insanity plea?"

Gray gave a quick nod.

Judge Bloom gathered up his papers and said, "Okay, let's get the show on the road." He looked at Rochelle Chandler. "Counselor, proceed with your opening remarks."

Chandler, looking competent and efficient in her dark gray business suit, got up from behind her table and walked over to the jury. "Good morning. During this trial we will present evidence and eyewitness testimonies that will prove to you that Barry Joseph intended to go into a Nation One Bank and threaten an employee at gunpoint. Now the defense will tell you that Mr. Joseph was distressed, and that might be true, but his actions endangered the lives of several people. Those same actions were premeditated and we will prove that beyond a reasonable doubt. When we are done, you will have no other choice but to declare Mr. Joseph guilty of all charges."

Chandler returned to her table and sat down.

"Your turn, Mr. Gray," Judge Bloom said.

Gray looked over at Barry who gave him a weak smile. Gray rose from the table, walked over and stood facing the jury. "Good morning, ladies and gentlemen. Ms. Chandler is correct about one issue: Mr. Barry Joseph was distressed and we will discuss that at length. We will be calling doctors and other experts in order to prove to you that Mr. Joseph was *not* in his right mind when he entered that bank. The defendant was being pressured by a big bully, Nation One Bank. This bully caused his credit to collapse. Because of his credit problems, his family could not fix problems they had with the house. His wife could not get a job because of their bad credit. Mr. Joseph did everything he could to cut his expenses, he even raised his deductible on his car insurance, which resulted in his being unable to fix his work truck properly after suffering an accident. My client's business was struggling to survive. My client could not get any response from Nation One when asking for a modification. He even hired a firm to talk to Nation One and then that company went out of business, leaving them in the lurch. Nation One did not even follow the guidelines set by the government, guidelines meant to ensure distressed homeowners were offered a fair modification. All Barry wanted was to stay in his home."

Gray stepped a few feet closer to the jury, paused for a brief moment, and then continued. "To top all this off, Mr. Joseph's mother was suffering from Alzheimer's and then his father died. It was just too much. He woke up that fateful morning and the world had changed. My client didn't scheme, ladies and gentlemen. He didn't plan. He acted on an irresistible impulse to try one more time to save his family from ruin."

CHAPTER 54

THE PROSECUTION called their first witness, Sue Bennett. Bennett stepped briskly over to the witness stand where she was sworn in. She climbed up into the witness chair.

Chandler strolled over to the witness stand and asked Bennett to tell the court about her background. Bennett explained that she had worked for Nation One for thirteen years. She'd been in the mortgage department for the last five years after being promoted from teller.

"Now, Mrs. Bennett. The last time Mr. Joseph entered the bank did he point a gun at you?" Chandler asked.

Leonard Gray stood up immediately. "Objection, Your Honor. Leading the witness."

"Sustained," Judge Harold Bloom said. "Rephrase the question, Ms. Chandler."

Chandler didn't hesitate. "Please tell the court what happened the last time Mr. Joseph entered the bank."

"He pulled out a gun and pointed it at me when I told him I couldn't help him."

Gray shifted in his chair at the defense table but stared straight at Chandler as if the answer didn't bother him.

"And what did he say after he pointed a gun at you?"

"He said no one would get hurt if I called someone in Corporate to work out a modification for his house."

"By Corporate, I assume you mean the corporate headquarters for Nation One?"

"Yes."

"And did you call someone in Corporate?" Chandler asked.

"Yes, Dan Evans, the vice president of the mortgage division in Chicago," Bennett said.

"Could you tell us how Mr. Joseph pointed the gun at you?" Chandler asked, suddenly changing the subject.

"Mr. Evans said he was not sure he could give him a modification, so Mr. Joseph there," Bennett said, pointing at Barry, "pointed the gun at me in a threatening manner. I was scared—he looked serious enough to carry out the threat—so I insisted Mr. Evans give him a modification."

"Let the record show that Mrs. Bennett identified the holder of the gun as Mr. Barry Joseph," Chandler said, looking at the jury. She turned back to the witness. "Thank you, Mrs. Bennett," Chandler said. She returned to her table. "I'm finished with the witness."

"Mr. Gray," Judge Bloom said, nodding at the defense attorney.

Leonard Gray smiled, rose from behind the defense table, and approached the witness stand. "Mrs. Bennett, could you please tell the jury what mood Mr. Barry was in?"

Chandler rose up out of her chair. "Objection, Your Honor. Mrs. Bennett is not a psychology expert, she's a mortgage banker."

"Sustained. Off to a rough start, Mr. Gray. See if you can do better," Bloom said.

Gray nodded. He knew better than to start off with a question like that, but he'd wanted to get a feel for Chandler's game plan. He cleared his throat. "My apologies, Your Honor." Gray turned back to Bennett. "Mrs. Bennett, was this the first time Mr. Joseph had ever been in your office?"

"No."

Gray proceeded with the line of questioning he'd planned. "When was the first time you saw the defendant?"

"About a year ago," answered Bennett.

"And what was the nature of the visit?"

"He requested a loan modification."

"I see." Gray turned back to the defense table and picked up a piece of paper. "Did Mr. Joseph tell you he had received a letter about seeing you for a modification?"

"Yes."

"And did he show you that letter?"

Bennett stared down at her hands, then looked back up. "I don't remember."

Gray walked over to the witness stand with the letter and confidently laid it in front of Bennett. "Isn't this the letter Mr. Joseph showed you that day, Mrs. Bennett? The letter you're not sure whether or not you saw?"

"Objection!" Chandler popped back up from her seat. "Leading the…"

"Denied." Judge Bloom looked at the assistant D.A. over his glasses, then glanced back at the witness. "Please answer the question, Mrs. Bennett."

"Yes, that is the letter."

Gray handed the letter to the clerk. "Your Honor, defense would like to submit said letter into evidence." Then he turned back to Bennett.

"What else happened that day?" Gray asked.

"I couldn't help him because he had already spoken with someone from Corporate on the phone"

Gray looked over at the jury with a raised eyebrow. "I'm confused. The letter stated that you could help him. Why didn't you?"

Bennett shifted in her seat. "You have to understand. Nation One is a large company. We send out form letters every day. That was a form letter. It didn't really mean anything."

The noise level in the courtroom rose as the audience started whispering. Judge Bloom tapped his gavel twice and the room quieted down. Gray waited until the room was quiet. "Then why in the world did they send Mr. Joseph the letter?"

"I don't know," answered Bennett, twisting in her seat. She gave the jury an apologetic look.

"What precisely was Mr. Joseph supposed to do when he received that letter, a letter that specifically stated he was to come see you about a loan modification?" Gray raised his voice, still looking at Bennett.

"Come in and see me, I guess." Bennett shrugged.

"And when he did that, you said you couldn't help him."

Chandler jumped up. "Objection, Your Honor. Asked and answered."

"Sustained. I think you made your point, Mr. Gray. Please move on."

Gray felt like he was on a roll. He nodded at the judge. "Mrs. Bennett, you said Mr. Joseph pointed a gun at you and Mr. Evans said he didn't think he could give him a modification."

"Objection, Your Honor. Asked and answered."

"Let me finish, Your Honor. I think Ms. Chandler is getting a bit jumpy."

"Denied. Proceed, Mr. Gray."

"Did Mr. Joseph get his modification?" Gray asked.

"No."

"Did the process ever get started?"

"Objection, Your Honor. This question has nothing to do with the charges," Chandler said, frustration evident in her voice.

The judge frowned. "Would both counselors approach the bench, please?"

Chandler walked toward the bench, stopping on Gray's right.

"Where are you going with this line of questioning, Mr. Gray? I have allowed you a lot of rope here and my patience is running thin." Bloom folded his arms and leaned forward, keeping his voice low.

"Your Honor, I am trying to establish my client's emotional state which is a key component of our defense. I think things will be made clear if you give me some latitude with this witness." Gray kept his voice low, but intense.

"Your Honor, I—"

Bloom held up his hand, stopping the assistant D.A. "I'll allow it, Mr. Gray, but you better get where you're going in a hurry."

"I will, Your Honor," Gray said.

"Okay, step away."

Everyone went back to their places and the questioning continued.

"Mrs. Bennett," Gray continued as if there hadn't been an interruption. "On the day of my client's most recent visit did Mr. Evans start the modification process?"

"Yes."

"But didn't you state earlier that Mr. Evans wasn't sure he could give Mr. Joseph a loan modification?"

"Yes, but..."

Gray cut her off. He'd made his point. A winning point at that.

"And yet, with a little encouragement, Mr. Evans somehow managed to get the process started. Is that correct?"

"Yes."

"How close did he come to finalizing the modification?" Gray clasped his hands behind his back and paced toward the jury box, then turned and walked back.

"The modification form had been notarized and was ready to fax over from the Chicago office for Mr. Joseph's signature."

"So Mr. Evans was, in fact, able to complete a modification?"

"Yes."

Gray walked over to the defense table, looked at his notes, and paused. He glanced at Bennett curiously and slowly strolled back to the witness stand.

"Did Mr. Joseph say anything about making payments?"

"Yes, he said he wanted to make payments."

"Now you have been in the banking industry for what was it…thirteen years?"

"Yes."

"Have you ever known anyone at a bank held at gun point by a guy asking for a modification—and also asking to make payments?"

Mrs. Bennett cleared her throat before answering. "No."

Gray shook his head. "Wow, Mr. Joseph gets a letter saying you can help him, but then you say you can't. Mr. Evans says he can't give him a modification and then he does. Wouldn't that make you pretty frustrated if someone lied to you like that?"

Chandler rose. "Objection, Your Honor. Is there a question in here or is Counselor merely pontificating?"

"I withdraw the question. No more questions at this time, Your Honor." Gray nodded to the witness, then walked back to his table and sat down, feeling pretty sure he had made his point to the jury.

CHAPTER 55

T HE SECOND DAY of the trial focused on expert testimonies.

"Ms. Chandler, please call your next witness," Judge
Bloom said with a wave of his hand.

Chandler looked down at her notes and stood behind
the prosecution table. This was her chance to disprove
the credibility of one of the defense's key witnesses.
She was going to nail this guy and nail him good.
"Your Honor, the prosecution calls Dr. Bartholomew
Jorgenson."

Joregenson got up and walked forward, touching
Barry's shoulder as he walked by. He took a seat in the
witness chair after being sworn in.

Chandler remained standing behind the table. She
glanced down at her notes again. Then she fixed

Jorgenson with a hard stare. "So, Dr. Jorgenson, do you know the defendant better than you know most of your other patients?"

"Yes, I do," replied Jorgenson. "The family goes to the same church my family goes to."

"I see. And did you see the defendant on a professional basis prior to the incident at the bank?"

"Yes, he came in just after his father passed on."

Chandler came out from behind the table, strolled to within five feet of the witness stand, and continued her questioning. "And did you prescribe something for the defendant at that time?"

"Yes," replied Jorgenson, looking over at Barry.

"What did you prescribe?" Chandler asked.

"Xanax, because he was overly anxious and having a hard time sleeping."

"What did he do or say that led you to that conclusion?" Chandler asked.

Jorgenson thought hard, trying to remember. "He said he was under a lot of pressure."

"Looking at your background, Dr. Jorgenson, it appears you were a surgeon and are now a general practitioner. Is that correct?"

"Yes" Dr. Jorgenson gave a quick nod.

"But nowhere do I see you have any background in psychology."

Leonard Gray immediately stood up. "Objection, Your Honor. Is there a question here?"

Judge Bloom frowned. "Ms. Chandler, I think I know where you are going. Please revise the statement into a question."

"I'm sorry, Your Honor. Mr. Jor...I mean Dr. Jorgenson. You are not a psychologist or psychiatrist, correct?" Chandler asked, giving the jury a look before turning back to the witness.

"No, I'm not, but..."

"No more questions." Chandler abruptly turned and went back to her table, feeling good about making her point.

Jorgenson appeared very frustrated.

"Your witness, Mr. Gray," Judge Bloom said, nodding toward the defense table.

Leonard Gray stood up and moved toward Dr. Jorgenson.

He stood quietly for a moment, apparently deep in thought.

"Mr. Gray," Judge Bloom said.

"Yes, Your Honor," Leonard Gray said. "Dr. Jorgenson, what exactly did Barry Joseph say to you during that appointment that indicated a prescription was necessary?"

"I believe his exact words were 'I just want to die'," replied Dr. Jorgenson, looking at Gray.

"Did you feel that he was suicidal?" Gray asked.

"Very much so. In fact, I told him to see Dr. Allison Daily, a psychiatrist."

"Do you know if he did see Dr. Daily?" Gray asked.

"No, I do not."

"Do you feel you did everything you could medically for Barry Joseph?" Gray asked.

"Yes, I do. I even called him the next day to see was how he was doing and told him again to follow up with Dr. Daily," Dr. Jorgenson said, looking over at the jury.

Gray started to walk away, then turned back. "One more question, Dr. Jorgenson. What is your background when it comes to psychology?" Gray asked.

Jorgenson smiled and looked relieved. "I minored in psychology in college and helped Dr. Robert Bartness during my tour in the Army. We dealt with the stress of combat."

"Did you see these types of symptoms in Barry Joseph?"

"Yes, I did," Jorgensen replied with a firm nod.

"Thank you, no more questions."

CHAPTER 56

THE WIND WAS coming off the Sierras and blowing all around northwest Reno on Tuesday afternoon. Tuesday meant the same thing for everyone in the neighborhood—it was trash day. Tess found the big green container and wheeled it over to the curb. She was startled to see Bob Dugan standing right behind her as she turned back to the house.

"Ahh! You scared me, Bob. I didn't see you there."

"Hi, Tess. I just wanted to know how you're doing without Barry being home."

Tess tried not to let her emotions show on her face. Barry had been in jail for way too long and the trial was on its fourth day. "It's pretty tough, Bob. I'm doing everything at the moment. I go into the store and work on the books and lead the workers where I can, but I'm not a hardware store owner. Barry is. Luckily, we have employees who love and care about us and the business."

"Very good, Tess. You're a strong woman."

"Hardly." At that moment the strain finally got to Tess. She started to shake uncontrollably, tearing up, and letting out a painful wail.

"Ah, Tess. It's going to be fine." Dugan put his hand on Tess's shoulder.

Tess wiped her eyes with the sleeve of her shirt.

"My husband is in jail and my kids are without their father. It is not fine!"

"I am so sorry for what happened, Tess. At times like these, it's good to remember that God will not give you more than you can handle," Dugan said, dropping his hand from her shoulder. "Look, the neighbors and I got together. We all love you and Barry. You're great neighbors and we…well…we wanted to do something." He reached into his coat, pulled out a large envelope, and handed it to Tess. "Here's a card from everyone in a two-block area. There's about three thousand dollars in there to help you out."

Tess stood there, staring at the envelope in her hand. She didn't know what to say. When she finally looked up she saw Dugan closing his front door.

Tess started to cry again, shaking her head in amazement as she walked back into the house.

Chapter 57

"**M**s. Chandler, would you please call your next witness?" Judge Bloom asked.

Tess chewed on her lower lip. According to Barry's attorney, this was the first of the prosecution's expert witnesses. Her stomach was tied in knots and it felt like a percussion band had taken up residence in her head. She almost hadn't come, but she couldn't stay away.

"Your Honor, I call Dr. James Cummins."

Dr. Cummins—a balding, seventyish man in a dove-gray suit—shuffled up to the witness stand and nodded as the judge swore him in.

Chandler had Dr. Cummins give a summary of his background, taking time to stress the fact that Dr. Cummins had graduated from Harvard and then spent thirty years working in the Johns Hopkins University

Psychology Department until his retirement three years ago.

Johns Hopkins. Tess took a deep breath. How could anyone dispute an expert from one of the premiere universities?

"So tell us, Dr. Cummins. Did you examine Mr. Joseph?" Chandler asked.

"Yes, and I found him a bit depressed but in full possession of his mental faculties," Dr. Cummins said.

"So you found him sane," Chandler said, looking at the jury. "Do you think Mr. Joseph may be trying to pull the wool over our eyes in order to get away with his stunt at the bank?"

"Objection," Gray shot to his feet. "Leading the witness."

"Sustained." Judge Bloom glared at the assistant D.A, then turned to the court reporter. "Strike the question from the record."

Chandler walked back over to her table, then turned to face the witness stand. "Dr. Cummins, in your professional opinion, was the defendant aware of what he was doing when he held Mrs. Bennett hostage at the bank?"

No, he wasn't, Tess said to herself.

"Yes." Dr. Cummins nodded. "In my opinion, Mr. Joseph was fully aware of what he was doing."

"On what do you base this conclusion?"

"Well, I gauged his reaction to a number of questions concerning the event in question, carefully monitoring his eye movements and body language in addition to his answers and his reactions to the questions themselves."

"No more questions." Chandler glanced at Gray as she sat down.

Leonard Gray straightened his jacket as he stood and walked over to the witness stand. He gave a slight smile as if knowing what the answer to his question was going to be.

"Dr. Cummins, how many hours did you spend examining my client?"

"Ten hours," replied Dr. Cummins.

"You know that my client is pleading insanity, or should I say 'irresistible impulse'?" Gray asked.

"Yes." Cummins nodded.

"Is it possible that in ten hours you could have gotten the depth and gravity of what my client went through?"

"I felt that two hours a day for five days was plenty of time, so yes," Cummins said, a confident tone in his voice.

"Dr. Cummins, is it possible that depression and stress can lead to insanity?" Gray asked.

"Well, I…"

"This is a yes or no question, Dr. Cummins. Is it a possibility?"

"Well, yes."

"No more questions," Gray said, straightening his jacket again as he sat down.

Chalk up one for the defense, Tess thought as she shifted in her seat. But was it enough?

CHAPTER 58

THE MORNING DAWNED rainy and chilly. The storm that swept in during the night would not let up. Street gutters started to fill. People couldn't help but get wet if they walked anywhere outside. In the Washoe County courtroom, a different kind of storm was brewing.

"Mr. Gray, please call your next witness," Judge Bloom said in his rough, authoritative voice.

Dr. Stedman Tanner was called to the stand. A chubby, dark-haired man sporting a beard and wire-rimmed glasses, Tanner strutted forward, looking every inch the professor in his black pinstripe suit.

Questions started with Dr. Tanner's background. Dr. Tanner had a doctorate in psychology from Stanford University; had interned at the Mayo Clinic in Rochester, Minnesota; and had worked at St. Mary's since coming to Reno. Without any objections from the prosecution, the testimony proceeded.

"Dr. Tanner," Leonard Gray said, gesturing at the jury box. "Could you please help our jury out here? What are some of the causes of insanity?"

"Other than physical deterioration or disease, stress and anxiety, along with other factors, are common triggers. A history of continuous exposure to stress can push a person way beyond the breaking point."

"You're talking about the kind of long-term pressure my client was suffering from?"

"Yes. I spoke with Mr. Joseph at length about his situation with Nation One. In my judgment, between trying to work out a settlement with Nation One and the effects of the economy on his business, Mr. Joseph has been under tremendous long-term pressure. This kind of prolonged stress has been proven to affect a person's outlook and behavior. Stress and anxiety are major factors in many cases of insanity."

Gray looked over at the jury to make sure they were all paying attention.

"Now, Dr. Tanner, could you please elaborate on how stress and anxiety can play with a person's emotions?" Gray asked, walking toward the jury box.

"Continuous exposure to stress can push a person beyond the breaking point and into insanity. As human beings, we try and fight to survive the stress and anxiety to keep our sanity intact; however, prolonged stress has been proven to affect a person's outlook and behavior."

"Please tell the jury what you told me about the part emotions play in cases of insanity," Gray said, looking at Judge Bloom.

Tanner nodded and continued, "As I've already said, stress and anxiety are major factors in insanity cases, but emotions play a key role as well. You see, emotions are closely entangled with health issues. Emotions can disrupt a person's thought process and make them engage in or do things they normally would not do. Emotions and feelings are so intertwined that they are major factors in pushing a person to the brink of insanity and beyond."

Gray approached Tanner and placed his hand on the witness stand. "Could Mr. Joseph have been pushed so hard he went temporarily insane?"

"In my opinion, the long-term stress that occurred during repeated dealings with the bank over several years, added to the passing away of his father and Mr. Joseph's resulting depression, was enough to push him temporarily over the edge."

"Thank you, Dr. Tanner. No further questions at this time."

Gray turned to the judge. "Your Honor, due to the fact that the state of my client's mental health is crucial in this case, I would like to reserve the right to recall this witness."

Judge Bloom gave a quick nod, then looked over at the prosecution table. "Your witness, Ms. Chandler."

Rochelle Chandler stood behind the prosecution table, straightened her blue dress, and approached Dr. Tanner as Gray headed back and sat down beside Barry.

"Dr. Tanner," Chandler said. "You sure seem know a lot about Mr. Joseph for a guy who just got in from LA."

"Objection, Your Honor. Is Ms. Chandler asking a question or badgering my witness?" Gray stood with an indignant look.

"Sustained. Ms. Chandler, play nice and ask your question."

"I'm sorry, Your Honor. Dr. Tanner, how many hours did you spend with Mr. Joseph?"

Tanner looked up at the ceiling. "I would say about… twenty hours."

"And it is your opinion that Mr. Joseph is insane?"

"Not now, but during the event in question, I believe Mr. Joseph was mentally unstable."

Chandler looked at the jury. "Now, Dr. Tanner, in this case wouldn't it be possible that Mr. Joseph used his reaction to his father's death to claim insanity?" She held up a hand as the doctor started to protest. "I'm not asking if the defendant *did* do this, I'm asking if it is possible."

Dr. Tanner shifted in his seat. "Yes, but—"

"Is it possible that the defendant could have misled you as to his state of mind at the time he was holding an innocent woman at gunpoint?" Chandler said, moving toward the jury box.

"Well, yes. It is possible."

"No more questions, Your Honor." Chandler strolled over to the prosecution table and sat down.

Gray leaned towards Barry and whispered, "I thought she'd pull this kind of crap." Then he raised his hand and stood.

"Your Honor, if I may redirect, I think I might be able to clarify some of Ms. Chandler's misconceptions."

"Proceed," Judge Bloom said.

Gray moved out from behind the defense table. "Dr. Tanner, please tell the court about your relationship with the LAPD."

"Objection, Your Honor, relevance," Chandler said, standing up.

"I'm just getting to the point, Your Honor. Relevance is in the answer if Ms. Chandler will just let me finish."

"Very well, objection overruled," Bloom said.

Chandler frowned as she took her seat.

Dr. Tanner continued, "The LAPD calls me in during suspect interrogations to help them determine if a suspect is lying or not."

Gray smiled, walked over to the jury, and asked, "And how many times was your assessment of these suspects proven correct?"

"We had one hundred and five convictions," Dr. Tanner said.

"Out of how many interrogations?"

"One hundred and seventy-six."

"Oh, so you listened to one hundred and seventy-six interrogations. How many times were you right in assessing whether the person was lying or not?"

"That would be one hundred and seventy-six times," Dr. Tanner said with a grin.

"And to satisfy Ms. Chandler's curiosity as to why you're in Reno, it isn't about this case, is it, Dr. Tanner?"

"Ah, no. I'm giving a lecture at the University of Nevada based on my fifth book about the body language and mental status of the lying patient."

"Thank you, Dr. Tanner. No further questions."

CHAPTER 59

THE NEXT DAY dawned cool and dry in the Truckee Meadows. The sun couldn't decide whether to hide behind the clouds or to shine. Everyone in the city was buzzing about yesterday's testimonies. The consensus was that the courtroom battle was like a boxing match. Every point made from one lawyer was like a punch to the other. The court gallery was anxious to hear the closing arguments from both lawyers.

Judge Bloom looked over at the assistant district attorney. "Ms. Chandler, your closing statement, please."

Chandler was ready. She had studied her closing statement until late last night. She was confident that she could convince the jury to convict the defendant as long as she made strong points. She rose from her chair, smoothed her dark maroon dress, and walked towards the jury box. She paced back and forth as she talked, stopping and turning when she wanted to make a point. "Ladies and gentlemen of the jury. You saw the weapon used by the defendant to threaten everyone at Nation One Bank. Barry Joseph went into the bank in broad daylight and pulled out a gun to bully Sue Bennett and the bank in order to get his way."

Chandler pointed at Leonard Gray. "Now, Mr. Gray over there wants you to feel sorry for his client. But we can't have every Tom, Dick, and Harry walking into a bank and pulling a gun just because they don't like the way they are being treated or because they are not getting their way. We don't let our own children push us around like that.

"No responsible parent lets their children have their own way. We give them rules. Just like this situation. The government sets the rules, and we, as a society, have to play by those rules. Barry Joseph walked into that bank with full knowledge of what he was about to do. Don't let him play all of you like a violin. Even the defense's psychiatrist admitted it was possible that he could have been misled by the defendant."

Chandler placed her left hand on the edge of the jury box and raised her right index finger in the air. "Lastly, think about something else. The Josephs entered into an agreement with Nation One. They signed papers entering into this agreement. When they figured out they were not getting their way, they wanted out of said agreement—somehow that agreement wasn't good enough. The bank held up their end of the deal, ladies and gentlemen. Why are they at fault?"

She moved to the other side of the jury box, turned and faced the jury. "You heard the prosecution's expert testify that the defendant is sane and went into that bank fully intending to hold an employee at gunpoint. His actions were premeditated. Therefore, ladies and gentlemen of the jury, you have no choice. It is clear you must declare Mr. Joseph guilty of all charges." Rochelle Chandler walked over to the prosecution table, sat down, and gave Barry Joseph a disdainful look.

"Mr. Gray," Judge Bloom said.

Leonard Gray sat at the defense table, deep in thought. He had to counter everything Chandler had just said or his client was toast.

"Mr. Gray," Bloom said a little louder.

Gray jumped, feeling as if he just woken up from a day dream. He stood and walked over to the jury box. "Ladies and gentlemen of the jury, Ms. Chandler did a great job of trying to make you think my client is a monster, a bully as she said. I submit that the only bully in this room is Nation One. This man and his wife have gone through hell trying to get the bank to talk to them. What more could they have done?"

Gray turned and stretched out a hand toward the defense table. "Then, just when things were almost as bad as they could get, my client's closest friend and confidant—his father—died. You heard evidence from our psychiatrist that this death was the proverbial straw that broke the camel's back."

He turned back to the jury. "Now I ask every one of you to think about something you really treasure." Gray paused a moment, then continued. "The Josephs treasure their house. It is not just a building made of cement, wood, and nails. Their house is their home. A place where Christmas is celebrated. Where the family gathers to celebrate and rejoice in living. The place where they are raising their children. They want to keep their home just as most of us do."

Gray moved from left to right and back again until he finally came to a standstill in front of the prosecution's table.

"Other home owners have had the opportunity to receive modifications. Many, in fact, did receive them. The Josephs wanted that opportunity and Nation One did everything in their power not to allow that to happen. You have heard testimony that no one at Nation One wanted to talk to them. You've heard about Nation One's lack of cooperation every step of the way."

Gray strolled over to the left side of the jury box, stopped, and faced the jury, using slight hand gestures to help him bring home every point.

"Barry Joseph's father taught Barry to stand up to bullies and that is exactly what Barry Joseph did. We all know what happened—in spite of their claims and denials—when directly confronted, the bank was able to give him the modification. They had the power to grant the modification all along. But like a big bully, they withheld what was within their grasp to give. Not only did they not grant the modification, they threatened to do what the Josephs most feared—to take away their home."

Gray moved just a few feet to the center of the jury box, still facing the jury. "The prosecution failed to talk about right and wrong. My client's father taught Barry the values of right and wrong at an early age. All Barry Joseph could see on the day he walked into that bank was that the bank was wrong and nothing was being done about it.

"The Josephs just wanted a chance. Why should the bank give modifications to some but ignore others? Such action is not fair and we all know it's not fair. You know it. I know it. The prosecution even knows it," Gray said, pointing at the prosecution table as he talked. "My client snapped and who can blame him after the way the bank treated his family? He was backed into a corner and like a cornered animal he reacted."

CHAPTER 60

f you didn't know what was going on in the Truckee Meadows area, you were probably living in a cave in the mountains. The coverage of the trial was on national TV, radio, and newspaper. Joseph v. Nation One was the talk of all the coffee shops, work water coolers, and hair salons. The Joseph trial was getting national attention with CNN, Fox News, ABC, CBS, NBC and other news outlets trying to outdo each other, featuring in-depth coverage of the events leading up to the trial. Emotions flared and everyone was on edge. Controversies popped up in both expected and unexpected places: rich versus poor, homeowners who'd paid off their homes versus those who had mortgages. And big banks—should we trust them or not? There were even people who didn't believe any kind of insanity was an excuse and thought the whole Joseph trial was a farce.

The aging marble courthouse fairly vibrated with the intensity. The jury felt the weight of their decisions. The deliberation had taken three brutal days. Judge Harold Bloom was feeling the pressure too. They were facing a no-win situation. He'd ended every day praying for strength, guidance, and justice.

The thirteen jury members took their assigned seats with solemn faces. This trial would impact the entire state of Nevada's home foreclosure crisis.

"Would the defendant please stand?" Bloom asked.

Barry stood up, feeling the butterflies in his stomach. He was worried sick. He didn't want to go to prison. Gray stood beside him. Barry put his hands on the table, steadying himself. His knees shook so hard he was sure someone would hear them clacking together.

Bloom looked at the jury. "Mr. Foreman, has the jury reached a decision?" Bloom asked.

Marvin Speaker struggled to his feet and nodded. "Yes, we have, Your Honor."

"What say you?" Bloom asked.

"On the charge of aiming a firearm at a human being, we find the defendant…guilty. On the charge of drawing a deadly weapon in a threatening manner, we find the defendant…guilty."

Barry's vision darkened. He took a deep breath and blinked hard. He looked over at Tess. She had her hand over her mouth. Tears streamed down her face. Barry was going to prison. The only good thing he could think of right now was his prison time would be limited. It wouldn't be for life. His heart skipped a beat at the thought of what could have been.

Judge Bloom nodded. "I'd like to thank the jury for their service. You are now dismissed. Sentence will passed two weeks from today." The judge rapped his gavel lightly on the bench.

Barry's stomach churned. He breathed deeply again, then turned and shook Gray's hand. "Thank you, Counselor. You did the best you could."

Gray nodded. "I'll talk to you tomorrow, Barry."

Barry looked back over at Tess and tried to smile. She wound her way through the milling crowd and gave him a big hug.

"I'll be all right," Barry said as the bailiffs took his arm and led him away.

CHAPTER 61

TWO WEEKS PASSED and Barry was sentenced to one year in prison. He was placed in a minimum security facility near Elko, Nevada.

All of northern Nevada was buzzing about the Joseph trial verdict and sentencing. Emotions were still running high. Many people felt sorry for the poor Joseph family, but Barry Joseph had to be found guilty of something — people couldn't just walk into a bank holding a gun and expect to get away with it.

Many homeowners who had never faced foreclosure were surprised and dismayed after learning about the tactics used by the banks, especially Nation One. Banks, especially big banks, began to be looked at with suspicion and distrust.

Withdrawals from big banks rose, followed by corresponding deposits in credit unions.

Nation One found itself facing a number of class action lawsuits when former employees finally revealed that they had been rewarded for denying modification applications and referring customers to the foreclosure department. Nation One denied all charges.

Spurred by the state attorney general, the state legislature enacted legislation requiring a bank to have all its paperwork in order before being allowed to start foreclosure procedures. Many judges asked to see the original bank note before approving foreclosures, but many of the banks could not produce the notes since they had been sold off as investments. This left many people waiting while the banks scrambled to find the appropriate paperwork. Foreclosures decreased from three hundred to ten in one month. Banks across the country reviewed their procedures, using their public relations departments to assure their customers they were doing their best to provide fair and equitable service.

Tess Joseph read the papers with a detached air. She still couldn't believe what had happened. It all felt so unreal. She watched Daniel and Sierra romping in the backyard, then looked back at the paper in her hand, rereading the latest *Reno Gazette Journal*. The headline declared that Nation One claimed they would cooperate with homeowners seeking loan modifications.

She shook her head as she reread the article for the third time. "I'll believe that when I see it."

EPILOGUE

One year and two months later…

IT WAS A HOT September Sunday. The temperatures around the Truckee Meadows were in the high eighties. The apples on the Joseph's Granny Smith apple tree were just starting to ripen. Tess stood looking out the back door of the family house, daydreaming of days gone by.

"Mom." Daniel held up a yellow slip of paper. "Can you sign this pass for me to go on a field trip? We're going to Carson City to see the State Capitol."

Tess frowned down at her son. "I thought you just went there."

"Mom, are you losing it? That was three years ago! This time we may even meet the Governor—we get to tour the Mansion." His grin spread from ear to ear.

Tess smiled. "Okay, okay. Get me a pen," she said with a sigh.

Betty smiled and tasseled Daniel's hair as he raced past her into the den.

Barry smiled at Tess from the living room. They'd ended up losing their house to foreclosure just before the laws changed requiring the appropriate paperwork to be produced by the banks. With Barry in prison and attorney's fees to pay, Tess hadn't been able to make ends meet, so they'd moved in with Betty. Barry's mother liked having family around her again. Barry enlisted the help of a few friends and Harold Frank supervised the addition of two new rooms for the kids—

The television announcer broke through Barry's thoughts. "The kick is up. It's...good! The 49ers beat the Lions thirty-two to thirty-one on a last-second kick!"

"Daddy...Daddy...look what I drew."

Maggie stood beside Barry's recliner, holding out a piece of paper. He forced his attention away from the TV. "What's this?"

"The painting I did for art class. Look at it, Daddy."

Barry took the painting, studying it closely. Something was off.

"Okay, Maggie. This is great, but..."

"You see, Daddy. This is our house now that we moved and there's Grandma and Daniel and Mommy and you and me," Maggie said proudly.

Barry nodded. "I can see that and above the house is the sun," he pointed, "and then a star up here in the right corner. Is this in the middle of the day or the night?"

Maggie giggled. "It's the middle of the day, Daddy."

"Then why do you have a star here?"

"Oh, that's Grandpa looking down on us. I couldn't forget Grandpa."

Barry grabbed his daughter and pulled her close to him in a huge hug. He swallowed hard, trying to speak past the sudden lump in his throat. "Oh, sweetie. You got that right. No one's going to forget Grandpa."

AFTER EVERYONE WAS in bed, Tess and Barry sat on the back patio, quietly enjoying a nice bottle of Mt. Vernon Zinfandel from Auburn, California. He told Tess about Maggie's picture. "I sure got a kick out of that picture."

Tess smiled, her lips soft in the glow from the living room.

Barry thought about the challenges they'd faced and how hard they'd fought to keep their house only to wind up losing it in the end. He'd realized something in prison—it wasn't the house he'd been worried about losing. It was his family. Just like Maggie's picture had shown. "You know, honey," he said after another sip of wine. "It is all about family, isn't it?"

Tess got up from her chair and snuggled close to him, giving him a quick peck on the lips. "Damn straight."

About the Author

Thomas Paul grew up in Iowa and Minnesota. He is a graduate of Minnesota State University of Mankato and has worked several years in marketing and television advertising. Paul currently lives in northern Nevada with his family, where he enjoys wine tasting, hiking, golfing, and following his favorite sports teams. Find out more at www.thomaspaulbooks.com

Useful Links

http://www.makinghomeaffordable.gov/pages/default.aspx

http://www.treasury.gov/initiatives/financial-stability/TARP-Programs/housing/mha/Pages/default.aspx

http://nevadahardesthitfund.nv.gov/

http://www.youtube.com/watch?v=hTsFjou22pc

http://www.biggerpockets.com/rei/foreclosure-process/

http://www.realtytrac.com/foreclosure-laws/foreclosure-laws-comparison.asp

http://www.loansafe.org/forum/us-bank-home-mort-gage/47031-being-referred-foreclosure.html

http://portal.hud.gov/hudportal/HUD?src=/topics/avoiding_foreclosure/foreclosureprocess

http://www.mbaa.org/files/ResourceCenter/ForeclosureProcess/JudicialVersusNon-JudicialForeclosure.pdf

http://www.huffingtonpost.com/anna-cuevas/home-affordable-modificat_1_b_3366049.html

Made in the USA
San Bernardino, CA
07 October 2013